CHOSEN

A DANIKA FROST PREQUEL NOVELLA

CONNOR ASHLEY
CHARLOTTE PAGE

inked entertainment

To my chosen sister, Chloe. Happy birthday!
- Connor

To my four-legged drafting partner, Lily. I owe you another round of fetch.
- Charlotte

At the edge of Greenvale, a small coastal town in the Pacific Northwest, Danika Frost sat beneath a canopy of sunset leaves, unaware of the panther stalking her like prey.

The beast was black as night, and if Dani had bothered to glance through the gaps in her picketed fence, she might have seen the glint of light off the creature's eyes as it prowled the edge of the tree line. Watching. Waiting. A low growl crackled through the trees, and Dani finally looked up from her reading.

But it was too late.

In two swift leaps, the panther soared over the fence, landing beside the girl, and snarled loud in her face.

Dani shrieked, her voice tearing across the yard, and dropped the college catalogue. She raised her arms to protect her head, just like her mother had taught her. But when pain didn't sink into her skin, she cautiously peeked through her fingers. "Kiva?" Dani groaned, dropping her hands. "You nearly gave me a heart attack."

The great feline licked the side of Dani's face. *You should pay better attention, Little Warrior.*

Kiva's voice was crystal clear inside Dani's mind, her tone soft and warm, much like her fur. Dani rolled her eyes, but she couldn't stop the smile playing at her lips. She loved Kiva, who in many ways was like a second mother, but Dani cringed at the term of endearment. She didn't feel like a warrior, and she worried she never would.

Dani picked up the college catalogue and brushed grass from the cover. Her fingers lingered over the image of students laughing while they studied on a perfectly green lawn. A forbidden hope rose inside, making her heart ache.

"We don't have to train *all* the time, Kiva. Most humans like to spend their weekends relaxing." Dani flipped the catalogue open to the section she'd been reading about the school's nursing program. "Besides, resting is all the rage with athletes these days."

Demons won't wait to attack simply because you're not in the mood, Kiva reminded her solemnly. *They won't wait until . . . what do they call it these days? Game time?*

"It depends on the sport, but no one calls it 'game time.'" Dani laughed, and Kiva blew out a disgruntled breath that tossed Dani's light brown hair out of her face. "Besides, I have you to protect me." She reached for Kiva, scratching behind the panther's ears.

Kiva rumbled low in her chest, as close to purring as her size would allow, and the sound reverberated through Dani. As the panther curled up beside her, Dani wished she could bottle moments like this and make them last forever. This was her favorite version of the two of them, but it was the one Dani's actual mother preferred the least.

"Danika?"

Speaking of mothers . . .

Andrea Frost stormed out the backdoor of their small rental home. Seeing her was like staring into a time machine. The Frost women shared the same pale skin, light brown hair, and dark eyes. Dani had inherited Andrea's nose and her full lower lip. But all the softness had been carved out of her mother, leaving only sharp angles and hard lines.

At the edge of Andrea's sleeves, black shadows billowed forth as the Ink on her arms dissolved, reappearing as fierce snakes at her feet. The python and king cobra shot ahead of Andrea and raced towards Dani while a raven circled above.

"Are you all right?" Andrea asked when she

neared, only seconds behind the ancient creatures that had appeared from her skin. "I heard a scream and . . . " She trailed off when she reached Dani, who was using Kiva as a pillow. Andrea sighed. "What is that?"

"What's what?" Dani asked, but her traitorous hands clutched the college brochure tight to her chest anyway.

"This." Andrea grabbed the stack of glossy catalogues sitting in a neat pile beside the tree. "I told you I wanted this nonsense out of the house."

"Technically, we're not *in* the house," Dani replied as the two snakes slithered up her arms and kissed her face with forked tongues, more like puppies than lethal serpents.

Come now, Danika, don't sass your mother. The raven swooped low and perched on Andrea's shoulder. The old bird fixed his black eyes on Dani. *You have a sacred duty—*

"To rid the world of demons. I know, Poe." Dani focused on his beaky face instead of looking at her mother. It felt easier to direct her plea at him. Poe was very expressive for a raven, but he was still a bird. He had never mastered the same soul crushing look of disappointment that her mother so often wore. "It'll be years before I carry the Ink. If I become a nurse, I can help people until it's my time."

Poe ruffled his feathers. *Four years is far too long to delay your training. No one in the Frost line has ever gone to college.*

"We could start a new tradition. Change doesn't have to be a bad thing.."

Andrea held up a hand, silencing both Dani and Poe before they could really get into it. "Poe's right, Danika. Our lives are too dangerous for you to lose that much training. I need you here with me, where you can learn as much as I can teach you before I'm gone."

"Mom . . . "

"I'm sorry, Danika, but my answer is final." Andrea nodded toward the house. "Now, come inside. I want to review your close combat techniques before I go hunting." Andrea smiled, her expression warming. "If you do well, I'll let Kiva stay home to keep you company."

Dani nodded, hugging her knees to her chest. "I'll be right in," she said and watched her mother leave as tears burned in her eyes. Only when she was alone did she let the tears fall. Only alone did she allow herself to feel the weight of her mangled dreams.

Even though it was her destiny to become the next Ink Carrier, to bear the ancient creatures on her skin, Dani didn't want that life. She didn't want the violence or the travel or the uncertainty that came with a life spent hunting demons. She wanted the future sprawling before her in the pages of the college brochures. She wanted green lawns and gothic architecture and terrible dining hall food. She wanted the consistency of spending four years in the same place. She wanted to study. To make friends. To fall in love.

She wanted to spend her life healing humans, not slaying monsters.

If only her mother could see that.

Dani scrubbed the tears from her face. She wouldn't give up on a real future, not without a fight.

She was, after all, her mother's daughter.

Dani sprang to her feet, her mind racing with all the ways she could try to convince her mother. Maybe she could compromise. There were two-year nursing programs. And scholarships. Dani could figure out how to pay her own way. There had to be *something* that would change her mother's mind.

With fresh conviction flowing through her veins, Dani hurried inside. They hadn't been in Greenvale long, only a few months, but it already felt like home. The single-story house was small, but it was the nicest place they had ever lived. Dani loved the beautiful white porch that wrapped around the front of the house. Poe liked to sit on the railing and drill Dani on the dozens upon dozens of different kinds of demons that had been spotted on the human plane, and the snakes liked to curl up and warm themselves on the stone steps on the rare occasion there was sun in their town.

Inside, Dani searched for her mom. Andrea wasn't in the kitchen, so Dani continued through to the living room, where her mother was weighing a pair of daggers in her hands.

"Good, there you are. Ready?" Andrea tossed Dani one of the knives.

Dani caught it out of the air, adjusting her grip on the hilt. "I'm going to college, Mom. With or without your blessing."

Andrea sighed and stared at the ceiling. Dani got the distinct impression that her mother was counting to ten before answering her, a trick Kiva had also taught Dani when she'd get frustrated as a child.

"I'd rather go with your permission," Dani said in a rush, wishing she'd taken more time to prepare. "I promise I'd still train every day, and I'd come back on all my breaks to learn more. Or I could go somewhere local. We could stay in Greenvale. There's a community college here. I could live at home and hunt with you at night. We can make this work."

"You know we can't stay that long, Dani. Once we've rid the town of demons, I have to move on." Andrea brushed a stray tear from Dani's cheek. "I get why you want to do this," she whispered, quiet enough that none of the Ink, who waited at the edges of the room, could hear. "But it's not meant to be."

"Please, Mom." Dani's voice wavered on the edge of breaking. "There has to be a way."

Andrea stepped back and adjusted her grip on the dagger in her palm. She glanced at the Ink. Kiva lay sprawled out in the door way, Jasper and Silas curled up beside her tail. Poe crossed the room and perched on the edge of the couch. Some silent message Dani couldn't hear must have passed between them, because finally, Andrea nodded.

"Fine." Andrea's single word sent a surge of hope ricocheting inside Dani's ribs. "If you can beat me, I'll let you go."

"Really?" Dani could hardly believe it, but before she could thank her mom, Andrea lunged forward.

Focus, Little Warrior! Kiva's voice filled Dani's mind. She dodged right, narrowly missing her mom's sudden attack. *Keep your guard up.*

Dani dodged and parried Andrea's attacks, the scrape of metal against metal pinging through the room as they drew together again and again. Dani pushed with all her strength, fighting for focus despite Poe's constant commentary.

For heaven's sake, Danika, stay on the balls of your feet. The bird flapped his glossy wings and let out an irritated squawk. *We just went over this!*

Leave her be, bird, Silas said, contorting his body to get a better look at the fight.

"If all of you . . . " Dani said, gasping for breath and spinning out of her mother's reach. "Could zip it. For just. A second." Dani lunged, striking out at her mother, but Andrea blocked her thrust. "I could actually—"

Dani's words were lost when her mother knocked the short blade from her grip, spun her around, and pressed her forearm against Dani's throat. With her other hand, Andrea raised the dagger and placed the tip just behind Dani's ear.

"You can't let anything distract you," Andrea said, her breath brushing against Dani's skin, which was now slick with sweat. "Even them. If you do, the demons will eat you alive." Andrea dropped the blade. "And I don't mean that metaphorically."

Dani shuddered.

"College isn't happening. I don't want to talk about this again." Andrea sheathed the dagger and rolled up her sleeves. "Kiva. Poe. Jasper. Silas," Andrea called to the Ink. "Return."

The four ancient creatures burst into black mist, visible only to the Carrier bloodline, and seared themselves into Andrea's skin. Dani's mom flinched as the Ink spread into a tattooed likeness of each warrior. The snakes, Jasper and Silas, along her forearms. Poe covered her neck and shoulder. Kiva claimed the whole of her back.

"Stings every time," Andrea muttered under her breath. She shook out her arms, like she could feel the weight of the ancient spirits' power in her skin, and reached for the leather jacket Dani had coveted all her life. "I have to hunt. Do you want to join me?" Andrea grabbed her sword—the one that had been passed down the Frost line for hundreds of years, the blade that would one day belong to Dani—and strapped it around her waist. "Well? Let's go."

Dani scrubbed hot, angry tears from her cheeks. "I hate you," she whispered, feeling the words all the way down to her bones. The truth of them. The terrible lie. "I will *never* be like you."

"Danika—"

But Dani didn't wait to hear whatever her mother wanted to say. She fled the house, leaving behind everything but the hollow, aching loss in her heart.

2

Dani wished she had brought a jacket, but even more than that, she wanted to take back what she'd said to her mother.

After she stormed out of the house, the sun wasted no time disappearing below the horizon. The autumn night was uncomfortably cool, and the lack of sleeves made Dani shiver. She crossed her arms, rubbing them to keep warm. At least the cold distracted her from the real reason she felt so miserable.

But she didn't want to think about that. Any of it. She couldn't face the future knowing the life she so desperately craved was always one step out of reach. And she certainly wouldn't let her mother's hurt expression linger too long in her mind. Dani knew she'd have to apologize, but she didn't know how she'd ever find the words.

A fresh breeze kicked up, making Dani shiver. She looked longingly into a coffee shop while she waited on the street corner for the lights to turn. The plush chairs looked like they'd swallow her whole, and nothing sounded better than a cup of steaming tea. Except perhaps a mug of hot chocolate with extra whipped cream.

Guilt swept through her for even thinking it. Poe would give her so much shit if he caught her drinking something like that.

Danika Frost, the squawking curmudgeon would admonish in his British accent, the affectation much thicker than the other Ink, despite all of them being in America since Andrea's great-grandmother left England. *Your body is a demon-killing machine. You can't fill it full of sugar!*

God, that bird was such a buzzkill.

Dani patted her pockets and sighed, crossing the street away from the coffeeshop. She didn't have any cash on her anyway. Not that they ever had much. Killing demons might be a full-time gig, but it certainly didn't pay like it. Her mom usually managed to find temp work in their new towns, and they had a little inheritance left from Andrea's mother, but they'd always lived simply. The Frost women never went hungry, but there was no room to splurge either.

"Danielle!"

The streets were mostly empty, so Dani knew the voice was meant for her, but she didn't turn around. She wanted to be alone, and besides, anyone who didn't know her well enough to know her name didn't warrant a pause. If they confronted her about it at school, she could claim she hadn't heard them.

Whispers chased after her, then another voice called out. "Danika?"

Begrudgingly, Dani slowed and glanced over her shoulder. A group of people from school were walking toward her. At the head of the group, his blond hair perfectly mussed, was Gabriel. A senior like Dani, Gabriel had something Dani never would: A normal life.

When the group reached her, Gabriel shoved his hands in his front pockets. A smile tugged at his lips, creating the cutest dimple Dani had ever seen. He rocked forward onto his toes and glanced back at the rest of his friends before settling his ocean eyes on her. "It is Danika, right? You're in my US history class."

Despite her best efforts, heat flushed to her cheeks. "Yeah, English and physics, too, I think. And Dani's fine. Only my mom calls me Danika." *And the Ink,* she added silently to herself. Humans like Gabriel didn't know anything about the demons that hunted them, and it was her job to keep it that way.

"Dani. Got it." Gabriel glanced at the assortment of classmates behind him. "We're heading over to the Haunt. You should come with us."

"Oh, thanks, but . . . " Dani trailed off, unwilling to share her penniless state but unable to conjure a better explanation with Gabriel's perfect blue eyes locked on hers. Even if she had money for the cover charge or drinks, she still shouldn't go. She needed to stay sharp. She needed—

No. Dani was *done* letting the Ink dictate her life. At least for tonight.

"A night of dancing sounds great actually," she replied, finding her voice again. She glanced up at Gabriel, her cheeks warming with embarrassment. "I sorta left home without my wallet though."

A cautious smile pulled at Gabriel's lips, too soft to show off his dimple again, but his cheeks turned pink. He rubbed a hand along the back of his neck. "You could come as my date," he said, nerves coating his voice.

"That'd be great." Dani shivered again and turned to let Gabriel lead her the rest of the way to the Haunt, a local under-21 club that most juniors and seniors attended on weekends.

Gabriel slipped off his jacket and handed it to her. "Here."

"What's this for?"

"You look like you're about to shiver right out of your skin."

Dani accepted the jacket and nearly cried with relief when she slipped it on. The fabric was warm from Gabriel's body heat and smelled faintly of whatever body spray he used. She was used to attracting attention—an occupational hazard for the new girl in a small town—but rarely did it come from sweet boys who were kind for no other reason than it was the compassionate thing to do.

As they headed toward the Haunt, Dani looped her arm through Gabriel's. His arms were deceptively strong, and the pink in his cheeks deepened to red. Dani let herself glance up at him. He was cute and uncomplicated, which was exactly what she needed after the day she'd had. Their small group walked the four blocks to the Haunt, and Gabriel paid for both of them to get inside and checked in the jacket Dani had borrowed.

The club was already in full party mode by the time they arrived. A live band played on stage—the posters proclaiming they were from the local college—and their speakers filled the space until it was impossible to hear the person next to you. The lights were kept low, making the world seem hazy and mystical. The pounding bass, screaming vocals, and packed dance floor pushed all thoughts of destiny and demons out of Dani's mind. She forgot about the fight with her mother. Forgot about the Ink. About Poe's lectures. Kiva's lessons. The hissing riddles of Silas and Jasper.

She forgot it all, until she was just a girl. Dancing with a boy. Their bodies pressed tight, moving in time with the pulse of the music. Gabriel's hands slid to her waist, pulling her close, and she wrapped her arms around his neck. He stared at her then, his shyness giving way to a hungry desire as their bodies moved together. She could feel it, the pull between them like a cord binding their hearts together.

Dani raised on her toes and kissed him.

He smiled against her lips, and then he was kissing her back. Hands everywhere. His tongue brushing against hers. He tasted of possibilities and endless summer, and Dani never wanted it to end. She hadn't meant for her first kiss to be like this, so wild and carefree, with a boy she barely knew, but in that perfect moment, she didn't care.

When Gabriel finally pulled away, breathing hard but grinning, he nodded toward the bar. "Want anything?"

At least, that's what Dani thought he said. She

nodded, not bothering to try to say anything at all. Her lips felt swollen. Her heart light. As Gabriel disappeared through the crowd, she let her fingers brush against her lips and wondered if she'd look different somehow. If anyone could tell she'd finally been kissed.

Gabriel's friends, most of them girls like Dani, pulled her into their tight circle. Dani let the music carry her away and let the goofy, embarrassed grin live on.

Across the circle, a tall lithe redhead suddenly jolted forward, scowling. A man stepped forward, catching Dani's attention. He ignored the way the girl pushed him away and wrapped his arm around her waist, letting his hand fall to her ass.

Anger bubbled up in Dani's chest, but she paused. Did the girl know this man? Were they just fooling around? But when the man leaned in for a kiss and the girl twisted her head away, Dani had seen enough. She closed the small space between them, grabbed the man's hand from around the girl's waist, and twisted it violently to one side.

The man cried out, his body bending in an attempt to reduce the angle on his wrist. The redhead slipped away from him, and Dani tugged hard, forcing the man's arm up behind his back. "Leave her alone, asshole," she growled in his ear and shoved him away from their group. She doubted he heard her words in the loud club, but the meaning should be clear enough.

He stumbled away, clutching his wrist, but he turned back to face Dani. His hard gaze traveled over her body, making her skin crawl, and then he stalked forward, a feral smile on his lips. This time, Dani didn't hesitate. As soon as he was in range, she punched him hard across the jaw. She may not have her mother's supernatural strength, but she'd been in training since she could walk. She learned to throw a punch before she could tie her shoes.

The man grabbed his face, blood already dripping from a split lip. He said something that looked suspiciously like *fuck you* before he stalked away.

Dani shook out her hand and turned around. Gabriel's friends were staring at her, mouths hanging open, but then the redhead flung her arms around Dani and hugged her tight. Dani froze, for just a moment, before she brought up her arms and returned the embrace.

"Thank you," she said, loud enough for Dani to hear.

Gabriel returned then with two glasses, the contents a deep red. "Making friends?" he asked, handing Dani one of the drinks.

She accepted the glass with a nod and a smile at

the other girl, but she was already turning to dance with the rest of her friends. Dani sipped from the slender straw, and the frozen drink burst on her tongue, a bright fruity concoction with just the faintest hint of alcohol. For a moment, she considered returning the drink and getting something that wouldn't muddle her head, but then Gabriel leaned in for another kiss, and she decided she didn't care. Not tonight. Perhaps not ever again.

Two glasses of the cold red drink and endless dances later, Gabriel pressed a kiss to Dani's temple. "Do you want to get out of here? I know this great diner down by the water."

Dani nodded, her head fuzzier than it should be. She waved to the rest of the group and followed Gabriel out the front door. He tried to give her his jacket again, but the cool ocean air felt amazing against her warm skin.

As they passed an alley, dizziness crashed into Dani like a wave. She stumbled, reaching out to catch herself on the side of a stone building.

"Are you okay?" Gabriel stepped closer.

Pain pounded in Dani's head, and she held up a hand. "I'll be fine. Just . . . give me a sec." She breathed deep and slow, trying to stop the world from spinning. She almost never drank, but she knew she shouldn't feel this poorly after only two drinks.

Unless— She turned to glare at Gabriel, who looked concerned and more than a little confused. "What did you put in those drinks?"

"Nothing. They had a little vodka in them, but not much. I swear." Gabriel's expression turned wary and he stepped back. "You're not going to puke are you?"

Dani shook her head, but inside, she wasn't as confident. The breeze picked up, scattering dried leaves down the sidewalk. The sounds intensified in her ears until Dani could hear the distinct scrape of each separate leaf on the pavement.

And just like that, all of her symptoms disappeared. Her vision stopped swimming. The pain in her head vanished. The unsteadiness of her stomach settled. She stood tall and inhaled deep. A flurry of scents assaulted her at once. Spilled booze. Piss. Gabriel's cologne. It was all sharper and more vivid than anything she'd ever smelled before.

What the hell?

"Are you okay?"

"Better than okay," Dani replied, smiling sweetly at him. "You said something about a diner?"

"Yeah, it's down this way."

Gabriel turned to leave, but as Dani started to follow, a searing pain shot across her chest. It skimmed along her neck and traveled down her shoulder. Fast, hot, and penetrating. Dani barely bit back the scream as she realized what was happening.

The Ink. Poe. Stitching himself into her skin.

Dani turned and bolted down the street, away from Gabriel. Away from the Haunt. Away from everyone. The world sped by, everything moving too fast. *Inhumanly* fast.

As the last of the Poe's Ink tore itself into her skin, Dani surged down an abandoned pier and looked into the calm waters, her terrified face staring back at her. She tugged down her shirt, afraid to see proof of what she already knew she'd find.

Black designs swirled across her skin in the shape of a raven.

No. No, no, no, no.

"Poe!" she cried, her voice tearing from her throat like a prayer.

The newly formed Ink bled from her skin, dark shadows pulling away and reforming into the ancient bird, the watcher of the skies. But it couldn't be. He couldn't be here. Not yet. Not so soon. Not unless—

"Where is she?" Dani demanded the moment shadows gave way to flesh and Poe ruffled out his feathers. "What happened?"

Follow me. Poe surged into the air. *Unless you want to become an orphan tonight.*

3

Dani raced across town, the stitch in her side and the ache in her lungs nothing compared to the agony of the ancient Ink searing into her skin for the first time. She followed Poe's skyward guidance, and her dormant Carrier strength and speed flooded her body, easing the fatigue in her muscles, making her feel like she could run forever and never tire.

. . . until Jasper burned down her left forearm. The king cobra twisted across her arm, imprinting from elbow to wrist. Dani barely held in her scream, and when Silas stitched himself into her right arm, his python form wrapping all the way up her bicep, she couldn't stop the whimper of pain that spilled past her lips.

She knew what this meant—Poe had said as much

—but Dani didn't want to believe it. She couldn't afford to, not when the last thing she'd said to her mother had been so cruel. Whatever was happening, Dani would save her. The Ink would return to where they belonged, and everything would be okay.

We're almost there. Poe swooped low, flying eye level with Dani for a moment before shooting back up into the sky. *Head into the cemetery!*

Dani followed as quickly as she could, but she stumbled just outside the gate, catching herself on the stone wall. She grit her teeth, but she couldn't hold back the heart-stopping scream as the final Ink stretched across her entire back.

Her back arched without her command, some primal instinct trying to avoid the pain. But there was no escaping. She remembered her mother's words and trembled with fear. *Stings like a bitch every time.* Tears clung to her eyes when she finally whispered the panther's name, calling her forth. "Kiva . . . "

The Ink shouldn't be able to appear so soon after being banished to a Carrier's skin, but something about the transference to Dani's body must affect their power. An almost unbearable heat slipped down Dani's back and pooled at her feet, rising into the form of her beloved Kiva. The panther's amber eyes held a grief so immense that it nearly crumbled the last of Dani's resolve. *Come, Little Warrior. Your mother needs you.*

Kiva growled and sprang into the cemetery without waiting for an answer, and Dani hurried to follow. Despite her increased speed and strength, Dani found it hard to breathe as fear took hold in her heart. Her shoes slapped against the stones, slick with damp and fallen leaves. As she passed old, crumbling mausoleums, screams pierced the night. The sound—feral and wild, like an animal near death—wrapped around Dani's spine, pushing her faster.

She followed Kiva around a corner and stumbled to a halt.

The scene unfolded before her in tiny details, her brain unwilling to look at the bigger picture. Her mom—Inkless and covered in blood—lay on the ground. Screaming. Eyes wide. Blood dripping down her nose.

A tall man with bone-white skin and ink-dark hair spilling down to his shoulders hovered over Dani's mother. He quirked his head to one side, the movement erratic and unnatural, but he had the most hauntingly beautiful face. A long, pointed chin. Thin nose. A smile that could freeze the sun. Beside her, Kiva growled, forcing Dani to look beyond the human trappings and see the demon within.

It was then she noticed his fingers.

They were easily three times the length of her own. The creature slid his index finger across his lips, painting them red with blood, and then plunged it into Andrea's skull.

Mother and daughter cried out, one with pain and the other with rage. The demon swirled his finger inside Andrea's skull, and she wept through her screams. The demon laughed.

"Let her go!" Dani sprinted as fast as her newly empowered body would take her and dove into the demon. Her shoulder slammed into his ribs and tore him away from her mother, his finger scraping against Andrea's skull as they went sprawling on the cold grass.

Andrea's screams faded to silence, and she lay as still as death on the dirt of a freshly covered grave.

Dani and the demon hit the ground hard, tumbling in a tangle of limbs. The cloying scent of dirt and sulfur and the coppery tang of blood filled Dani's senses. When the world stopped spinning, she found herself on her back. The demon sat perched above her, a toothy grin on his long face.

"What's this?" the demon hissed, trailing his long, blood-slicked finger down her face. He leaned close, pressing his face into her neck to inhale deep, like Dani was some rare vintage of wine. "Ah," he said, sounding delighted. His wet tongue slid up her neck. "The very last of your line. And so young, too."

The demon leaned back and wrapped his long fingers around her throat. Dani stared up at the terrible beauty of him. His features were ageless, both young and old all at once. His porcelain skin perfect and smooth. His dark hair falling in silken sheets past his chin.

But the eyes . . . Each time he blinked, there was a moment when she could see their true color. Burning red irises that gave way to the false human blue. Poe's lessons came back in a rush. Red eyes. Pale skin. Fingers long enough to scramble your brain. This wasn't just any demon; he was the worst of their kind and twice as rare.

He was a reaper, stealing souls to make them his own.

The fingers around her throat tightened. Spots dotted Dani's vision.

"I'm going to enjoy this," the demon crooned in her ear, his voice like the crashing of waves on the shore.

Do something! Poe cried from above, preparing to dive.

A roar erupted on Dani's left. A blur of shadow and heat charged toward them, tearing the demon away from Dani. She turned in time to see Kiva land on the reaper, her jaws snapping. The thin man caught Kiva's shoulders before she could sink her mighty teeth into him.

Get up, Danika. On your toes, just like we taught you! squawked Poe just before he dove at the demon, scratching out with his talons.

Dani tried to stand, but her whole body trembled. She squeezed her eyes shut and tried to fight the fear that paralyzed her. "Jasper. Silas. I need you."

Slippery shadows coiled down her arms, dripping from her fingers, and soon the giant snakes were whole again, dashing across the grass. The demon shoved Kiva away, the panther's back slamming hard against the corner of a headstone. The granite shattered under her weight.

Fingers wrapped around the back of Dani's neck, lifting her up until her toes skimmed the ground. She hadn't even seen the demon move, but he was already behind her, squeezing hard enough to break her neck. Her earlier rage rose up again, boiling like acid. She was *not* going to die like this.

Silas! Jasper! She called out to the snakes with her mind as the demon choked away her breath. The Ink moved quickly, spiraling their massive bodies up the demon's legs and chest, squeezing until he could no longer keep hold of her. His fingers went slack, and Dani fell to the ground. Her body reacted on instinct now, rolling out of the demon's reach and springing up to her feet.

Above them, Poe let out a fierce cry and attacked. The raven scratched at the man's face, and with each slash of his wicked talons, he tore away the glamour, revealing more of the demon within. Pointed teeth. Blood-red eyes.

The reaper screamed, a frustrated, terrifying sound. He grabbed Silas, pulling the python from his leg, and tore him in two.

"No!" Dani screamed as the now-familiar burn worked down her right arm, the spirit of Silas returning to her skin to recover. The demon shouldn't be able to do that. He shouldn't be strong enough to destroy the Ink so easily. Fear sprouted from Dani like roots, pinning her in place. She watched the black Ink spread across her skin, and in her distraction, she didn't see what the demon did to Jasper, but soon he was etching into her skin again, too.

Dani squeezed her eyes shut. This couldn't be happening. It wasn't real. She had to be dreaming. She—

The sword, Little Warrior. The sword! Kiva lunged at the demon and dug her teeth into his shoulder, black blood running from the wound. The reaper shouted, more angry than hurt, and grabbed for the giant cat, hurtling her away like she was little more than a new kitten. Poe dove again, fluttering his wide wings, blocking Dani from view.

She turned and searched the graveyard, looking for the flash of silver among the leaves. *There!* She turned and ran, leaving the Ink to fend for themselves. A pained squawk sent her heart racing, and soon Poe was burning into her chest and shoulder. She was failing them. All of them.

A moment later, the agonizing pain of a thousand blades exploded against her back as Kiva joined the rest of the Ink on her skin. The shock of it sent Dani sprawling, her fingers inches from the hilt of the sword.

Cold hands grabbed her ankles, pulling her away from her only weapon.

"Enough of this," the demon growled. "I've worked too long to have your cursed family ruin my plans." With a jolt, he flipped Dani onto her back, standing to his full height and looking down his long nose at her. "I wanted to take my time, but I'm tired of your little games, human."

Dani scrambled back, the dirt and stones cutting up her palms as she moved. Reaching. Stretching. Just a little further . . .

The demon lunged, his fingers stretching to long, needle-like points.

Her grip curled around the hilt.

She swung.

The blade sang through the air, slicing clean through the monster's wrist. His hand fell onto her chest, and Dani tossed it away as the monster screamed. He clutched his bleeding arm to his chest, eyes blazing red. "Don't think you've won anything, young Carrier. You've already lost." And with that, the reaper disappeared in a cloud of sulfur smoke.

Dani allowed herself a moment of relief, staring at the severed hand that rested on the grass a few feet away. She didn't know what she'd do with it without Jasper or Silas to consume the demon's flesh and banish it back to the lower realms. But then Dani remembered her mother, and she scrambled back to her side. "Mom? Mom, it's me. It's Dani. Wake up." She shook her shoulders, and when that didn't do anything, she felt her neck for a pulse.

There. It was weak, but it was there.

"Poe? Kiva? Silas. Jasper." She called to the Ink, but nothing happened. Tears burned hot in her eyes. They must still be too injured to take form in her world. Too depleted from their battle.

"Mom, *please.* You have to get up. You have to be okay."

Andrea's eyes fluttered, and Dani's heart gave a little lurch. Her mom's eyes opened fully, and the relief was so strong it physically hurt. But then confusion creased Andrea's brow. She scrambled away from Dani.

"Monsters," she mumbled, her voice shaking. "Monsters everywhere. Danger and screaming and it's the end, the end, the end."

"Mom?" Dani reached out, but her mother shrank way, covering her ears with her hands.

"It's the end. I hear the monsters. They're so happy. Laughing, laughing, laughing."

"Kiva," Dani called again, desperate for the panther's guidance. Still nothing. "Silas," she tried. He was banished first. Maybe he could help. "Silas, please," she begged, and the Ink on her right arm shuddered then released, pooling before her.

Silas curled on the ground, moving sluggishly as he lifted his head, looking between Dani and Andrea, his forked tongue flicking out to taste the wind. Andrea screamed when she caught sight of the mighty python.

"What's wrong with her? What did he do to her?"

Her mind is no longer her own. She isn't fit to bear the Ink. Silas turned away from Andrea and curled up Dani's leg, nudging her hand with his head. *We are now your burden to carry.*

4

One year later.

ani was late.

She always seemed to be late these days, always lacking *something,* with no shortage of people—or *birds*—to tell her so. She didn't spend enough time hunting. She didn't earn enough money at her job. And she definitely didn't come *here* enough. She hated this place. The walls were a soft cream, freshly painted and accented by soft, gauzy photographs of foliage.

At the front desk, Dani signed her name, trying not to think about how long it had been since she visited. One week. Maybe two?

"It's nice to see you, Miss Frost," the woman behind the desk said, her smile sickly sweet. "Do you remember the way?"

Dani nodded and slipped down the hall without a word. It was hot, almost stiflingly so, but Dani didn't take off her leather jacket. It was the only thing of her mother's that fit her, the only thing that remained of their life in Greenvale. Besides, she didn't need anyone seeing the uniform underneath. At room 113, she paused in the doorway and took a deep breath, steeling her nerves. Dani never knew what she'd find in this room.

Slowly, her shoes squeaking on the linoleum floor, she entered.

"Mom?"

Her voice was a whispered, barely there thing. She found Andrea asleep in her bed, as she so often was these days. Relief clutched Dani's chest, followed swiftly by shame. Neither emotion was particularly helpful, but Dani couldn't prevent herself from feeling either of them. It was always so much easier when her mother was asleep, even if thinking so made her a terrible daughter.

Dani sat in the chair beside Andrea's bed. The hallways were decorated with bats and pumpkins for Halloween, but Andrea's room was bare of decorations. "Hi, Mom." Dani traced the edge of the soft blanket. She didn't know how much her mother heard, but she tried her best to pretend everything was normal. "I have good news. I found a new place to live. I have the best view in the entire city. You'll love it."

They'd travelled a lot in the first few months after Dani took on the Ink. She'd dropped out of school and taken her mother east, trying to track the monster who did this. Who stuck his demonic fingers into her mind and ruined everything. They kept on the road, relying on Andrea's meager savings, then stolen credit cards, to get what they needed to survive.

But life on the road was hard on all of them, especially Andrea. She'd press her face to the window and rant unintelligibly about monsters. When they stopped for supplies, sometimes she'd refuse to leave the car, and more than once, she tried to make a run for it. Dani was faster and stronger than ever before, but something about the way Andrea moved made it hard to keep hold of her. At night, as they'd stop at run-down motels to sleep, Dani would push her bed in front of the door so her mom couldn't escape.

When they finally made it to Blackthorn, a city so full of demons that even Poe agreed it would take years to get rid of them all, Dani tried to make a life for them. She rented a tiny apartment and went looking for work. But she was always away. Working. Hunting. As far as Poe was concerned, she was never hunting *enough.* So, she increased her patrols.

Blackthorn, she quickly learned, was the demon summoning capital of the world.

Dani tried leaving her mother home alone, but after she trashed the place twice, she left Silas behind to babysit. That ended with Andrea screaming until the landlord keyed into the trashed apartment to find the mythical python wrapped around Andrea, tying her to a chair.

They were evicted that same night.

It didn't help that they were already two months behind on rent.

In the end, it was Kiva who suggested this place. Somewhere doctors could keep an eye on Andrea. Somewhere she'd be safe so Dani could fulfill her duties as the Ink Carrier. In the two months since, she'd learned everything she could about the five families of necromancers who seemed to run the city. She'd destroy every last one the demon summoners if that's what it took to find the monster who ruined her life.

"I'm going to find him, Mom," she whispered then, reaching for Andrea's hand. "I'm going to kill the demon who did this." And maybe, just maybe, whatever twisted magic had hurt her mother would be undone.

"Miss Frost?" The deep, rumbling voice of Andrea's doctor greeted Dani from the doorway. "Could I have a word?"

Dani stood and pressed a kiss to her mother's forehead, who stirred but didn't wake. When she turned and saw the doctor's drawn face, worry joined the shame that burned her skin. "What's wrong? Is she okay?"

The doctor, a man in his late forties with dark hair that grayed around the edges, plastered on a pleasant smile. A patient one.

"Your mother's condition hasn't responded to any of our usual medications. The best we've been able to do for her is keep her mildly sedated."

Andrea's *condition* had been diagnosed as a severe case of schizophrenia, but though the symptoms might look the same, Dani doubted medication could undo what the demon had done.

"Have there been any other . . . " she trailed off and had to clear her throat before she could continue. "Any incidents since the last time I was here?"

"Not since the escape attempt we called about last week." The doctor checked the chart in his hands. "The injuries were minor, but we did have to increase her dosage after that."

Dani nodded. She didn't need to ask who had been injured in the attempt — it was never her mother. Always a nurse or another patient who got in her way. A doctor she mistook for a demon.

"I'm sorry, sir." Dani was always apologizing these days. To her mom. To the people who were paid handsomely to care for her. An alarm beeped on her phone, and Dani stifled a groan. If she didn't hurry, she'd owe another apology to her boss Frank for constantly being late to work. Dani glanced up at the doctor, who hadn't stepped aside to let her pass. "Was there something else?"

The doctor nodded. "There's the matter of the bill. The card we have on file was declined."

"There must be some mistake." Dani glanced back at her mother's sleeping form. She was growing restless. "I used the card last night. It was working fine." She reached for her phone. "I'll call the bank and see what's going on."

The doctor shook his head, stalling her hand. "This is the second time the card has been declined. You'll need to see reception to run payment." He smiled at her, but it was a pitying thing. "I asked them to waive the late fee, but this is the last time. Understood?"

"Of course. It won't happen again." Dani held her breath until the doctor took his leave. When she gave herself permission to breathe, her knees almost gave out beneath her. She was out of money. Out of options. Her mother needed this place, but it cost more than she made. Leaving her less than nothing for herself.

She had to find the demon and reverse what he'd done.

She needed her mother.

Dani hurried down the hall and slipped past reception without stopping. She'd find the money somehow. She had to. For now, she had a job to do.

Just not the one she was destined for.

The crisp air blew across Dani's sweat-slicked face, tossing her faded red hair over her shoulders. She needed another dye job, as soon as she could afford one of the cheap store-brand boxes. She slipped out of her jacket, the black leather too warm even in the cool October air. In the shadows, she called Poe's name, and the bird soared from her skin. All of the Ink were restless against her flesh, but Poe was the only one who wouldn't draw attention.

It's been too long since they went hunting, Danika, Poe said as he stretched his wings against the sky. *You have to make time for them.*

"I know," she muttered, but there wasn't anything she could do about it.

She was late. Again.

Dani stepped out of the shadows and continued down the street, the deep mustard yellow of her shirt glaring back at her from the windows of brightly lit shops. The inviting smells of the restaurants made her stomach growl. Spicy Indian fare. Savory Italian sauces. Even the greasy pizza joint made her mouth water.

"Dani?"

She kept moving. No one in this city knew her. She was hundreds of miles from anywhere she'd ever been before, which was part of what she liked about Blackthorn.

"Danika Frost?"

Shit.

The young man broke into a grin when she turned, deep dimples burrowing into his cheeks. He looked familiar, with his crystal blue eyes and blond hair, but Dani couldn't immediately place him. "Can I help you?"

"We went to Greenvale High together, remember?" He paused, but Dani shook her head, still at a loss for the boy's name. "I'm Gabriel," the man said, and in a flash, Dani remembered. He'd been there that night at the club. They'd danced. She'd even kissed him.

"Oh my god, Gabriel! Of course! How have you been?" She faked excitement like it was her job, like it was the only thing keeping her alive.

"I've been great! What about you? I almost didn't recognize you with the red hair and everything. I haven't seen you since . . . " He trailed off, either unsure exactly when he'd seen her last or embarrassed by the memory of their dancing. Of their kiss. Or, more likely, the way she had ditched him in the middle of the street when she'd run off to save her mother.

"Yeah, sorry about that night, by the way. My mom got this amazing new job, but we had to get all the way out here, like, immediately. She needed me home to start packing right away. But hey, we both made it to Blackthorn. Small world, right?" Dani knew she was rambling, knew her explanation didn't really account for the way she had disappeared, but she didn't know what else to say. She gestured vaguely around her, as if to suggest she lived among such sparkle and wealth.

Gabriel shook his head. "Damn, that must have sucked, switching schools part-way through senior year."

She shrugged. "I survived." But in reality, Dani

hadn't finished school. She'd left Gabriel's hometown and spent the twelve months since killing demons and bouncing from one shitty apartment to the next. "What brings you this far east?"

"College. I'm in the bio program at Blackthorn University, pre-med track. Got a full ride." He beamed at her, but this time, as jealousy slammed into her so fiercely it made her teeth ache, she couldn't muster a smile in return.

Boys like Gabriel, whose family made more in one month than Dani could in a year, didn't need full rides to college. Dani was sure his family had a college fund all saved up, and now he wouldn't even need to dip into it. He was going to be a doctor, without a penny stacked against him, while Dani could barely keep a roof over her head and food in her belly. The unfairness of it all, of everything she sacrificed to keep sweet, dimpled boys like Gabriel safe, threatened to crush her. When she forced herself to glance up at him, there was an expectant look on his face.

"I'm sorry. What?" she asked when she realized he was waiting for a response.

"I asked if you're going to B.U., too. It's a big campus, but I haven't seen you around."

The bitter truth sprang to her lips. That she couldn't afford college. That her mother never wanted her to go at all. But she couldn't get into all that, not unless she wanted to fall apart in front of someone who was more of a stranger than a friend, despite the kiss they'd shared.

"Oh, no. I'm actually taking a gap year to travel. I'm just in town visiting my mom for the weekend." Dani crossed her arms, rubbing her cool skin. Now that she was standing still in the autumn wind, goosebumps had formed on her flesh.

Gabriel glanced down, taking in the yellow shirt. Dani followed his gaze, the transparency of her lie burning her face. The logo of Frank's Diner, the rundown grease pit in the heart of the city's poorest neighborhoods, stared back at her. It was the only place desperate enough to hire someone without any experience.

Her abilities as the Ink Carrier meant she never dropped a plate, but it didn't do much for her *poor attitude*, as the establishment's titular Frank often complained.

"Right. Well, it was nice to see you." Gabriel was backing away now, pointing over his shoulder, as eager as she was to be done with the charade. "We should get together sometime. Maybe go out for coffee."

"Sure."

But he was already gone, his words hollow. He

hadn't even asked for her number, so he had no way to get in touch. Not that she wanted him to have it. She didn't need a shiny example of all the things she had longed for and lost.

Dani checked her phone and cursed. She was *really* late now.

She slipped her leather jacket back on and hurried down the street. The bright lights of downtown gave way to dirt and decay. Trash littered the gutters, and the air smelled like piss and stale beer. Overhead, Poe squawked and Dani could already hear the lecture spilling off his beak.

He landed up ahead, resting on a low-hanging branch.

You're late.

She glared at him as she passed his tree. "I know."

Frank isn't going to like it.

"You don't even like Frank. What do you care?" Dani's stomach growled again. She was famished, but she'd need to put in at least three hours before she'd earn a free meal during her break. Another grease-soaked hamburger and limp fries.

Poe made an indignant sound and flapped after her. *If you insist on working this pitiful job, the least you could do is be punctual.*

"Do you have another idea to keep her safe?"

Dani didn't have to say her name. Poe knew

exactly what she was talking about. He finally went quiet.

"Unless demon hunting starts pulling in some cash, this is the best I can do."

What she didn't say, what she didn't want to admit to anyone, *especially* not the judgmental raven, was that her best might not be enough.

5

Frank's Diner, despite its dingy exterior and peeling vinyl seats, was a popular place in Blackthorn. The food was cheap and it was damn delicious—if it wasn't the only meal you ate most days. The staff was down two waitresses that night, which meant Dani wasn't getting a break anytime soon, no matter how much her stomach grumbled.

Though she knew she shouldn't, Dani stole a fry or two from most of the plates she delivered, anything to keep her on her feet and moving. The nagging hunger clawed at her ribs, a pain rivaled only by the stiff smile she kept plastered on her face.

By the fourth hour, the faces at the tables were starting to blur together.

She lost track of the coffee requests and simply

gave up, serving everyone the stale decaf that no one ever ordered. Hour after hour she carried trays of burgers, breakfast foods, and Frank's famous meatloaf.

A busboy turned abruptly and crashed hard into Dani. She managed to hold onto her heavily-laden tray of food, but the boy's plates went flying. Bits of leftover food littered the floor, and the remnants of someone's strawberry milkshake splattered over the front of Dani's shirt.

"Are you fucking kidding me," she snapped, staring down at her ruined uniform. *Right* as her boss came through the swinging kitchen doors.

Frank Mancini was a giant of a man. In his late fifties, he towered well-over six and a half feet tall. His back rarely stood completely straight—the toll of three decades spent working the flat top, grilling all manner of meat and cheese and thick bread—but he was still an imposing man. One eye was always open a little wider than the other, and his gray hair had grown wispy on top.

"Danika Frost," he bellowed. His voice cut through the music that poured from crackling speakers, making Dani cringe. "You watch that mouth of yours."

"Fuck. No, shit. Gah! Sorry," she said quickly and continued to her table. Frank helped the busboy clean up his mess, but no one seemed to care that Dani had prevented six full meals from being lost to the grime-covered floor. And *she* wasn't the clumsy one who started the whole chain reaction in the first place!

She pushed down the frustration and focused on her table, where a group of rowdy high school seniors had already finished their second round of drinks, each clamoring for a refill as she tried to deliver their meals. Two bacon burgers, one with extra bacon. A double stack of pancakes. An order of chicken fingers. And a pair who had decided to split the entire menu of appetizers—mozzarella sticks, buffalo wings, and three kinds of fries with the works.

They were probably going to skimp on the tip, too, the little shits.

Dani placed the half-dozen empty cups on her tray and hurried into the back. She dumped them by the sink and slipped into the employee bathroom, scrubbing the sickly-sweet ice cream from her shirt. The heavy makeup she wore around her eyes had gone smudgy and uneven from sweat, and she did her best to clean up the lines with a bit of wet paper towel. Her stomach groaned as she worked. She was starving and had agreed to skip her break to keep up with the understaffed dinner rush. The universe was cruel to leave her sticky and cold, too.

When she was done, her makeup looked half-decent and her shirt was soaked, but at least most of the ice cream came out. She gathered up a fresh round of drinks and delivered them to the table, at which point the seniors asked for three different dipping sauces and one boy, with a thin, patchy mustache, threatened to send back the burger if he didn't get more bacon.

As if she didn't have other tables to deal with.

By the time the six teens left, leaving a measly two-dollar tip, Dani's patience had worn thin. At least the diner had calmed and another shift of waitresses had shown up to help.

Dani finally stole a moment for her long overdue break and sat alone in a corner booth. She picked at the remains of her turkey club. The lettuce was wilted and the tomato unripe. It was gone too fast, and already she could feel herself getting hungry again, but she still had another hour left in her shift.

The door chimed as another patron walked in. Dani glanced up, checking to see if the newcomer looked like a good tipper. She needed a healthy tip after dealing with cheap students all night. But instead of the well-to-do adult she was hoping for, there was a kid standing before the hostess, holding up a photo.

Something about the desperate look in the girl's face had Dani on her feet and moving forward. As she approached, she reassessed her initial assumption.

The girl was probably thirteen, maybe fourteen, but she'd looked smaller from a distance. She wore a knit hat over her head. At first, Dani assumed the girl's parents were overcautious about the chill, but then she noticed the girl's missing eyebrows. Her thin, almost frail frame.

"Are you sure you haven't seen her?" the girl was asking the hostess when Dani got close enough to hear over the racket of other patrons.

"I'm sure. We haven't seen her," the hostess replied. "Do you need a table or—"

"Can I show the photo around?"

"Hi there. Can I help with something?" Dani interjected before the hostess dismissed the girl outright. She knew Frank's policies. Diners were not to be disturbed under any circumstances, and she could see the refusal in her coworker's eyes.

"You know the rules, Dani," the hostess said, warning in her tone.

"I'm on break." Dani recognized the kind of desperation that burned bright in the girl's eyes, felt it echoing back all the ways she'd felt lost and alone since her mother's attack. She knew then, if there was any way she could help, anything at all, she would do it. "Come with me."

The girl, who stood a full six inches shorter than Dani's five foot four, followed Dani to the corner booth where her plate and drink still sat. There were a few leftover fries, which Dani offered to the girl, who introduced herself as Cassie.

"What brings you out to Frank's Diner at this time of night?"

The girl slid the photo across the table. A young woman, probably in her early-to-mid-twenties, stared back at her. She had beautiful golden-blonde hair that fell in soft waves to her shoulders. Her smile was genuine and warm, and she had her arm around a smaller version of Cassie, who sported matching blonde locks that fell to her waist. "This is Lana," Cassie explained. "She's my sister."

Dani noted the catch in Cassie's voice, but didn't know what the younger girl wanted her to say. "She looks just like you."

Cassie pulled the photo back and turned it to face her, her fingers trailing along the edge of the picture. "She's missing," she said at last, fat tears spilling down her cheeks. "She's been gone for two days, but she's been acting weird for weeks."

"What kind of weird?"

Cassie scrubbed at the fallen tears. "I don't know how to explain it. She's different. Like, she normally plans things out weeks in advance, but all of a sudden, she acting super impulsive. She stopped reminding me to take my meds, and she started bringing strangers to the house, a different person almost every day."

"Maybe she got tired of being responsible and wanted to party. It happens." But a sick feeling worked its way into Dani's chest. The Ink stirred against her arms and back.

"Lana's not like that. She always used to brag about how normal she was, like it was cool to be so boring." Cassie scoffed and rolled her eyes, like this was an argument the sisters had often. But then the moment passed, and Cassie pressed the heels of her hands into her eyes to ward off fresh tears. "Lana's not the kind of person who breaks rules. I swear, it's like she's allergic to it or something. But the day after she dyed her hair, she had us dine and dash from her favorite restaurant."

"Huh, that is weird," Dani said as neutrally as she could. Diner patrons had only skipped out on her check twice since she'd been there, but each time had been absolutely crushing, especially since Frank took the bill out of *her* paycheck.

"But that's not even the weirdest part. Lana ordered a burger. *Rare*." Cassie put so much emphasis on the reveal, but Dani just stared at her, confused. "Lana's vegan," the young teen clarified. "She won't even eat honey from humanely raised bees or anything. But then all of a sudden, she's eating this bloody burger? Something is seriously wrong."

"And now she's missing on top of everything else," Dani mused, tapping her fingers against the table. The signs were all there. The reckless behavior. Changes in routine. An appetite for all sorts of flesh. But how could she tell this girl her sister was probably possessed?

"Have you tried the police?" Dani asked.

Cassie shook her head. "No! And you can't tell them. If they find out my sister is missing, they'll throw me in foster care until they find her. Maybe even forever, if she keeps acting so weird."

"What about your parents?"

"They died when I was ten." Cassie picked at a fry from Dani's plate instead of looking at her. "It's just me and Lana."

"Shit, I'm sorry kid." Dani pressed her fingers into her temples and massaged her aching head. "We have to do *something*. You need someone who can watch out for you and warn you not to wander in neighborhoods like this after dark." Dani drummed her fingers against the table again. Even though Cassie didn't want the police involved, she wouldn't get that choice forever. If Lana's disappearance was demonic in nature, the chances of reuniting the family were practically nonexistent.

"Wait," Cassie said, sitting up straighter. "*We?* You'll help me?"

Dani hadn't made a conscious decision to help, but as soon as Cassie asked, Dani knew she couldn't say no. She understood the pain of becoming your own parent too young, and Cassie couldn't be more than fourteen, at least three years younger than Dani had been. "Yeah, I guess I am."

"Oh my god, thank you!" Cassie scrambled out of the booth and threw her arms around Dani, hugging her tight. "Here. Give me a pen." Cassie grabbed a napkin and scribbled her phone number and address for Dani. "Can you come tomorrow?"

"Yeah. I'll make it work." Dani glanced at the address. It was in a nicer part of town, the kind of place her mother might have picked if she had brought them there. If she wasn't locked inside a hospital for her own protection. A rush of emotion threatened to drown Dani. She swallowed it as best she could.

Frank came out from the kitchen and shot Dani a warning look, tapping the spot on his wrist where a watch would sit if the old cook bothered to wear one. Dani sighed and slipped out of the booth. "Let's get you home."

Dani called Cassie a cab and walked her out, handing over the last twenty in her wallet to make sure Cassie got home safely. "Call me if your sister returns," Dani said, wishing she had a safe place for the young teen to crash while her sister was gone.

She wasn't too worried about the potential demon —if there was one, it already had plenty of time to hurt Cassie. If it hadn't hurt her yet, it most likely wouldn't. But Dani didn't want Cassie spending another night in an empty house, scared and lonely and lost in her own thoughts. Dani didn't even want that for herself, and she had four ancient beings to keep her company. "Are you sure you're all right alone tonight?"

"I'll be fine. And I'll call if I hear anything from Lana. I promise." Cassie said, and when the taxi rolled up, she hugged Dani again. "We can do this, right? We'll find my sister?"

Dani opened the cab door and offered the girl a smile. "We'll do our very best."

Poe was waiting for Dani at the end of her shift. He hopped from branch to branch before taking off into the air. *You smell like bacon grease*, he griped.

Dani rubbed her sore shoulders and didn't dignify the raven with an answer. The sun had fully set, and the lights of the city blotted out the stars. Dani was struck with a sudden, aching desire to lie in the cool grass and chart the constellations with her mom. She missed the full-bodied dark sky that could only be found in the middle of nowhere. In the city, you could never escape the light. Not fully.

She shoved the wanting aside and walked toward her apartment. The weight of the snakes at her arms made her already exhausted body even more weary. They wanted to come out. They wanted to hunt.

"Silas. Jasper." She whispered their names like a prayer, and though it would burn when they returned to her skin, the relief of their anxious energy bleeding out of her was almost enough to make her cry. In the dark, she could barely make out the snakes as they dropped to the sidewalk at her feet, shadows solidifying into strong scales and lithe bodies.

When are we hunting? Jasper asked, his hood flaring as he slithered across the cracked and crumbling cement. *I'm hungry.*

Jasper was always hungry. Silas, too. The pair could tear a demon in half and swallow it whole in less than a minute. They'd get their chance, just not tonight. "Soon," Dani promised.

Above them, the raven let out an irritated sound. Poe swooped low, the wind from his wings brushing against Dani's cheeks. *Soon? What do you mean,* soon?

You have to hunt, Danika. This wretched city will be overrun if you don't take your duty seriously.

Dani scowled. Blackthorn was overrun long before she'd ever gotten there. "I've had a long day, Poe. I can't hunt safely when I'm ready to collapse."

Poe landed softly on her shoulder and nuzzled her cheek with his beak. *Regular hunting will keep your strength up, Danika. You can't keep putting it off to work in that grease pit.*

"I know." Dani brushed the soft feathers on Poe's chest, soothing herself as much as him. "But I can't tonight. I just . . . I can't." She dropped her hand and squeezed her eyes tight. "I don't know what else to do. If I don't find a way to earn more money, Mom can't—"

Shhhh . . . Silas hissed, shrinking in size until he was no larger than a garden snake. He slithered up Dani's body and wrapped around her wrist. *Ignore the Bird. He does not speak for all of us. We will be fine until you can hunt again.* He flicked his tongue against Dani's palm.

"Thanks, Silas," she whispered, wincing when he returned himself to her skin, burning into her like a thousand tiny cuts. Before Dani could recover from the sensation, Jasper seared into her other arm, neither snake lingering in the physical world without an impending hunt to entice them.

Reptiles, Poe grumbled and took off into the night. He never liked when the other Ink contradicted him, especially when they were right.

While Poe flew overhead, Dani's thoughts circled back to the girl she'd met at the diner. She had a bad feeling about Cassie's missing sister. While there might be a thousand human reasons for the strange changes in Lana's behavior, so much of what Cassie described sounded like possession. And a fresh one, too.

In some ways, new possessions were the most dangerous. The demon inside didn't yet know the limits of their body's capabilities—often hurting themselves or others in those first few weeks. The demons were reckless in the human world, often too excited to be in the mortal realm to understand the need for caution.

Dani was still trying to piece together a plan for her meeting with Cassie when her apartment rose before her. The ancient brick facade mirrored the rest of the block, each building in danger of crumbling to dust. Dani yanked open the rusted front door and started the five-story climb to her apartment. On the third floor, Poe returned to his place along Dani's chest and shoulder, bringing with him a low, constant thrum of nervous energy.

She sucked in a breath, gritting her teeth against

the pain of his return. The skin on her chest was always the most sensitive, and it didn't help that his presence was also the most draining. By the time she reached the fifth floor, Dani was ready to collapse. And instead of the silence and warmth she so desperately craved, the drafty building was a cacophony of unending noise. Old gameshows played too loudly by the elderly woman who lived at the end of the hall. Simulated gunfire and foul-mouthed taunts from a neighbor playing video games late into the night. False orgasmic moans from the camgirl next door.

At her own apartment, Dani fumbled with her keys and let herself inside, locking the several deadbolts behind her. There wasn't anything to steal in her apartment, and she could certainly handle herself, but the last thing she wanted to deal with was another human.

On the rickety side table, Dani dropped her keys and ignored the stack of mail she'd let pile up. Almost all of them were stamped with the dreaded *FINAL NOTICE* warning in vivid red ink.

The apartment was far smaller than she'd described to her mother, with a tiny window whose only view was the brick wall of the next building over. The cramped studio held little more than the mattress on the floor and the small table covered in bills. She didn't have a couch, television, or even a table or a single chair. The most impressive piece of furniture was the one thing she'd brought all the way from Greenvale: a hand-carved wooden chest, filled to the brim with weapons.

The sandwich at the diner was a distant memory at that point, so Dani flipped through the cupboards, careful of the one with the broken hinges. She looked through her meager supplies and settled on a cup of instant ramen that she'd gotten on sale—four for a dollar—and filled the kettle with water from the sink.

Dani turned on the kettle and her whole apartment went dark. She glanced at the stack of *FINAL NOTICE* envelopes, pressure building behind her eyes. Of course, they picked today to cut her power. Of *course,* it had to be before she could eat. Dani gripped the kettle and flung it across the room, letting loose a blood curdling scream that anywhere else would send neighbors into a panic.

Here, she was just another unfortunate soul.

The kettle slammed into the wall on the far side of the little studio, denting the dingy gray walls. It shattered on impact, water raining down.

All over her mattress and her only set of sheets.

Dani's legs gave out, and she crumbled to the floor. "Kiva," she called pitifully, and the panther uncurled herself from Dani's back. The great cat stared back at Dani, golden eyes gleaming, and licked the tears from her face.

Without either of them needing to say a word, Kiva sprawled on the floor, creating a makeshift bed. Dani curled up beside her friend, the closest thing she had left to a maternal figure, and cried herself to sleep.

6

Dani woke the next morning with the sun on her face and the world gently rising and falling beneath her. Kiva still slept soundly, the panther's breath gently rocking Dani. She glanced at her ancient flip phone and groaned when she saw the time. It was almost eleven. Way later than she'd wanted to start the day.

She hurried through a frigid shower—her water heater lost with the rest of the electricity—and returned Kiva to her back before she finished getting dressed. Kiva's return hurt the longest, the Ink covering the entirety of her back, but at least her energy was soothing.

When she was finally ready, Dani headed for the subway.

Cassie's place was too far to walk, otherwise she wouldn't waste the fare. At least being so late meant she had missed rush hour. When Dani emerged from the subway, she found herself in one of the nicer areas of town. Not wealthy by any stretch of the imagination, but people here owned small single-story houses. They had tiny patches of green lawn out front, which was more than could be said about Dani's shithole apartment building.

Dani counted the mailboxes until she reached Cassie's address, where she found a small yellow house with white trimmed windows. The lawn hadn't been cut in a week, and the white paint had gone dingy with age, but it was blessedly quiet on the street. A thread of something akin to nostalgia wove up Dani's spine, clinging to her ribs. At first, she couldn't figure out why, but then it hit her in a rush—this was so much like their small home in Greenvale, where the last thing Dani had said to her mother was how much she hated her.

Before she could knock, there was a rustle at the window and the door flew open. Cassie stood on the other side, hatless, displaying her completely bald head. "You actually came." The young teen seemed surprised, though pleased, to see Dani on her doorstep.

"I keep my promises, kid." Dani stepped into the house, taking in the warm lived-in feel of the place. The furniture looked old, but it was all there. A couch and loveseat in the living room, complete with a TV on an honest-to-god entertainment center. Pictures lined the walls, most of them of Cassie and Lana, plus some of an older couple. It was immediately clear they were Cassie's parents, sharing the same bright blonde curls.

"Would you like the tour?" Cassie asked, standing awkwardly in the hallway.

"That would be great. Could we end in your sister's room?" Dani figured that's where she'd find the most clues to Lana's odd behavior.

Cassie brightened. "Definitely." She led Dani through the kitchen, which was immaculate and stocked full of food. Dani longed to grab one of the apples on the counter, but she didn't dare ask.

On the fridge, someone had posted a calendar full of hand-scribbled notes. *Appointments*, Dani realized. Chemo dates. Doctor's visits. Nutritionists. On the counter, there was a giant pill case, organized for daily morning, noon, and evening meds.

"Why are these all crossed out?" Someone had taken a red marker and drawn an X through all the up-coming appointments on the calendar.

Cassie folded her thin arms against her chest. "I decided not to go anymore."

"I'm sorry," Dani said, and she truly was. Cassie was so young, and there was so much life in her eyes. So much vibrancy in her skin. She didn't look like a girl on death's door, though if the calendar was any indication, she clearly was. "Do you mind if I ask what's wrong?"

"Cancer," Cassie said with a shrug, not bothering to clarify. "It's Stage IV and basically everywhere now. The chemo wasn't doing anything except make me feel awful. If this is the end, I want to go out having fun, not so tired I can't do anything." She grinned, a small, fleeting thing. "Lana's been helping me apply for that wish making thing. We want to visit Disney before I go."

"That'll be really fun." Not that Dani had ever been to any kind of amusement park. Her mom hated them. She always joked that even demons knew better than to brave those kinds of hideous crowds, especially in the Florida heat.

Cassie dove into an explanation of all the amazing attractions she wanted to see and the rides she wanted to experience, but Dani started to question her earlier instincts. Maybe this wasn't a demonic possession at all. Maybe Lana's erratic behavior was simply grief over the impending loss of her sister. A ticking clock could lead people to do strange things.

"Can I see her bedroom?" Dani prompted, cutting Cassie off in the middle of a macabre story of people illegally sneaking the ashes of loved ones in Disney parks in order to spread their remains. Cassie wanted Lana to do that for her, but Lana refused since it was something the park expressly forbid.

"Right! Sorry. This way." Cassie led Dani down the hall and stopped before a closed room. "I haven't been in there. I'm not supposed to . . . "

"I won't make a mess. Promise."

Dani rested her hand on the doorknob, a tremble of unease fluttering across her skin. She blew out a breath, rolled out her shoulders, and stepped inside.

The room was nothing like Dani expected. Unlike the rest of the house—which was clean and neatly organized—Lana's bedroom looked like a sexy tornado had blown through.

Skimpy lingerie littered the floor, many of the pieces still with tags on them. Handcuffs hung from each side of the headboard, and there was even a strap-on peeking out from underneath the bed. Dani scanned the rest of the room and tried to ignore the rest of Lana's . . . toys. Suit jackets and slacks were balled up in the corner of the room, almost like they were shoved out of sight, while dresses with low plunging necklines draped prominently over the backs of chairs.

"Does your sister party a lot?" she called to Cassie, who was still hiding out in the hallway.

"She never used to."

"What about dates? Does she have a boyfriend or girlfriend or anything?"

An awkward silence stretched between them. Then finally, Cassie's small voice called from the hallway. "She's been going out a lot recently. She always tells me not to wait up for her."

"Hmm . . ." Dani continued her search, looking for something that would point her in the direction of Cassie's missing sister. "What does your sister do for work?" Dani went through the discarded suit jackets, checking the pockets for any clues.

"She was an assistant at an accounting firm."

"Was?"

"They fired her a few days ago." The awkward pause came again. "She didn't say why exactly, just that they were too stuffy and didn't know how to have fun."

"Does your sister have any problems with drugs or alcohol?" Dani came up empty with the pockets, finding nothing more than a few stray receipts and sticky notes with grocery reminders on them.

"No, nothing like that."

Dani reached for the last pair of slacks, and something sharp poked into her thumb. She withdrew a sturdy black card and flipped it over, silver glinting in the light. She ran her thumb over the raised letters. The Ink stirred against her skin. Dani grinned.

They had hunting to do.

7

*O*bsidian.

Dani leaned against a stone building down the street from the nightclub and glanced from the silver lettering on the card to the neon sign above the entrance. There was a wrongness in the air, and the Ink stirred anxiously against her skin. They wanted out, which usually meant demons were close by.

Even from half a block away, music pulsed loud enough to penetrate Obsidian's heavy black doors. The tall windows were all covered with thick curtains, blocking all view of whatever debauchery happened within. Though Dani had never been inside before, she knew the club's reputation.

Owned by one of the five necromancer families that ruled Blackthorn, Obsidian was a place where desperate humans could get anything they wanted—for a price. Fame. Fortune. Beauty. Love. Power. There were no limits at places like Obsidian, so long as you were willing to pay in blood.

Dani adjusted the waistband of her skin-tight black jeans and smoothed the front of her shirt. She'd sacrificed one of her favorite soft tees, slicing through the collar to lower the neckline, and paired the entire ensemble with her leather jacket. She approached the front door, worried for a moment they'd ask for ID, but the bouncer waved her inside. *I guess necromancers aren't worried about underage drinking.*

The pounding bass shook through Dani's bones, making it hard to think. The place was *packed* with bodies, and she bristled when she realized not all of them were human. She spotted the first demon behind the bar. He looked normal enough at first, a handsome Black man mixing drinks and dancing to the music. But when he turned to grab a straw, Dani spotted the long tail curling up toward his shoulders.

Instinctively, Dani reached for the sword she kept strapped to her waist when she went hunting, but her fingers came up empty. She'd left her more conspicuous weapons at home. Dani scanned the club, the Ink itching terribly at her skin, but she couldn't bring them out here. To her growing horror, the longer she looked, the more demons she spotted among the crowd. Though normal humans wouldn't see the imperfections, Dani catalogued them all.

A young white woman with a forked tongue.

A pale man with flame-red hair and cat eyes.

On one of the raised dancing platforms, a Latina woman danced with abandon, spreading her near-translucent wings.

Everything inside Dani told her to run. To get the hell out of there and regroup. She should call the Ink, wait in the alleys outside the club and pick off the demons one-by-one as they left. But Dani had a missing woman to find, so she forced her racing heart to calm the hell down. She needed to act natural.

She scanned the club again, letting her body move in time with the music. Of the people who looked human, there was no telling how many were necro-mancers. She'd never actually met one before, but she'd heard enough from Poe to keep her distance. She and the Ink had sent hordes of demons back to the underworld since they'd arrived in Blackthorn, which made them terribly unpopular with both demons and the necromancers who raised them.

The song ended, and for a moment, the club was plunged into darkness. A few excited screams echoed around her, but then the beat of a new song pulsed through the space and spinning lights lit up the room.

Dani shook her head, disgusted by the humans

who came to this place, trading their souls for short-term gains. Who willingly pressed their fragile, mortal bodies against demon-possessed corpses.

A violent shudder worked up Dani's spine, and she headed for the end of the bar, as far away as she could get from the tailed-demon she first spotted. At least at the bar she could sit and observe in peace while she searched for Lana.

One of the dancers jostled Dani's shoulder as she tried to slip past, and her Ink burned against her skin, desperate to attack. Dani glanced back at the retreating form. The man turned, his eyes flashing an inhuman shade of purple. *Not a man*, Dani corrected herself, scowling at him, *a demon.* The creature must have been inside the dead body for a few weeks, maybe even several months. His movements were calm and sure, and he didn't seem to have a problem keeping composed around so many potential victims.

Poe's righteous anger burned against Dani's chest, and for once, she fully agreed with the raven's pushy emotions. He wanted to peck out the demon's violet eyes, and Dani longed to let him. Now wasn't the time, but soon each and every demon in attendance would taste her blade.

When Dani finally reached the bar, she ordered a simple water with lemon. She couldn't afford to have booze altering her reactions. And, frankly, she couldn't afford to pay for the alcohol anyway. As she sipped her drink, she ran through what Poe had told her about the five families that ran this city. They were politicians, business executives, crime lords, and even religious leaders. The Dasari family managed the city's nightlife. Most of their clubs catered to humans, but a few—like Obsidian—specialized in arranging deals between willing humans and the demons eager for a way into the human realm.

"What's a pretty thing like you doing in a place like this?" Hot breath accompanied the soft words in Dani's ear, and webbed fingers trailed along her neck as the intruder brushed her hair over one shoulder.

She turned, and the demon behind her smiled, exposing pointed, fish-like teeth. Her hands curled into fists, but before she could break the creature's nose, a new figure blocked her view, coming to stand between them.

"What did I say about touching patrons without their permission?" The man's voice resonated in his chest, commanding authority. Dani hated him immediately. Only a necromancer would speak so firmly with a demon.

The demon shrank back from the reproach. He raised his hands, those slimy webbed fingers waggling in surrender. "Fine, fine," the demon whined, "I'll find someone who wants to play."

Once the demon had stalked off, the man turned to Dani, a very human smile lighting his features. His long dark hair was pulled into a low bun; a few shorter pieces had fallen out to frame his face. He had beautiful brown skin and the warmest brown eyes Dani had ever seen.

The man, who seemed to be of Indian descent, looked Dani up and down. The polite grin on his face turned genuine, and far too cocky for Dani's tastes. "Sorry about him. We have very strict policies about consensual . . . *dealings* in this club."

"I'm sure you do," Dani replied, turning back to her glass to hide the sarcasm in her eyes. Necromancers only played at fairness, but their business relied on humans not understanding the full weight of what they were bargaining away.

"You know, a 'thank you' is customary in these sorts of situations."

"I didn't ask for your help, nor do I need it." Dani glanced at the man, assessing him in much the same way he'd assessed her. He was at least half a foot taller than her and probably a few years older, too. His body was trim, the shape and curve of his muscles evident in his tailored suit.

"Huh. True enough." One of his thick, well-manicured eyebrows raised up his forehead. "Well then, can I buy you a drink to make up for ruining whatever riveting conversation you were about to have?"

Heat burned Dani's cheeks as the man leaned closer and gestured for the bartender. He wore some kind of crisp cologne that probably cost more than two months of her rent, but she couldn't deny that it was an intoxicating scent. It reminded her of first snow and sunset leaves. She wanted to get lost in it.

"I'm Raj, by the way."

"Danika." She responded without thinking, Raj's closeness muddling her usual caution.

"Well, Danika, what brings you to Obsidian?"

The bartender arrived, giving Dani a reprieve from Raj's attention. She turned back to the crowd, scanning the dance floor. And there, in the middle of it all, was the reason she'd come to the damned club in the first place.

Lana.

8

The woman dancing at the center of the club had all of Lana's features but none of the reserved, cautious personality that radiated off the photographs in Cassie house. This Lana was wild and carefree, her blonde hair in loose curls down her back. She wore a short skirt and skimpy top, dancing with a man who had one arm wrapped around her bare waist while he pressed kisses down her neck.

Lana glanced up, as if she could feel Dani's gaze trained upon her, and smiled. Long canines pressed into Lana's lower lip, but she returned her attention quickly to her dance partner, turning around to kiss the man. When she finally pulled away, Dani noticed the faintest shimmer to the air, as the demon fed on the man's sexual energy.

Dani stifled a groan.

Cassie's sister was possessed by a succubus.

Though she'd never faced one herself, she'd overheard her mom and Poe complaining about succubi a few times. They weren't uncommon demons, but they were damn irritating. Succubi were rarely satisfied with merely sucking the sexual energy from their victims. They liked to toy with humans like a cat might taunt a mouse before eating it.

On the plus side, they often left their victim's alive . . . which boded well for the man currently grinding his crotch into Lana's ass, but if he was currently in a monogamous relationship, he could kiss that goodbye. There was nothing a succubus liked more than watching relationships implode around them. They loved chaos, and had a habit of causing it wherever they went.

Dani accepted the drink Raj had bought her and slammed it down in one gulp. Alcohol burned against the back of her throat, but the liquid courage should make her night suck a little less. She stood from the barstool and stalked toward the dance floor.

"You're welcome!" Raj called after her, but she simply flipped him off without turning around. He may be hot, but he was still a necromancer. She didn't owe him anything.

The music of the club pulsed over her, and Dani

let the thud of the bass work into her bones. It rattled up her spine, bouncing from rib to rib as she let her body sink into the rhythm. Soon, she was no longer a demon hunter, her limbs no longer made for chasing monsters or gripping ancient swords. She was an extension of the *thud, thud, thud* of the dance music, her hips swaying to the beat.

Keeping Lana in her sights, Dani moved from one dance partner to the next, letting the most human-looking men hold her close, their bodies moving as one in the cramped nightclub. She shut off her brain, letting her body do whatever felt good, pretending the men beside her actually gave a shit about who she was. Dani let herself become lost in desires she normally kept locked away, pent-up feelings the succubus inside Lana wouldn't be able to pass up.

Lana glanced up from her dance partner, scanning the room until her gaze locked on Danika. A wicked grin split the monster's face, her canines even longer than before. The *wrongness* of her expression, the proof of her demonic insides, was invisible to the human in her arms. Only those touched by the paranormal—other demons, necromancers, and hunters like Danika—could see the creeping evil, the cracking of humanity.

Dani pretended not to notice. She stumbled forward, acting clumsy with alcohol and entranced by

Lana, who subsequently abandoned her current partner and met Dani on the dance floor.

"I haven't seen you around here before," Lana purred, her voice husky and seductive.

Dani's cheeks grew warm despite herself. She fluttered her lashes and glanced up at Lana, faking a nervousness she did not feel. "It's my first time."

Her words seemed to please the succubus. "Care to dance?"

A simple nod from Dani was all it took to reel Lana in. The succubus tugged Dani close, and soon the pair were dancing, the crowd parting around them. Even though she'd mentally prepared for the demon's tricks, Dani felt herself falling under Lana's spell. A hand at her waist. A brush of lips against her neck. And always moving, moving, moving as the music enveloped around them. But then Lana's fingers brushed over the Ink on Dani's skin, and a cold shiver brought her back to her senses.

She leaned in close to Lana, her lips brushing the other woman's neck. "I know what you are."

Lana laughed. "And what is that? A delight? A fabulous lover? A—"

"A monster," Dani finished instead, pulling back to watch Lana's reaction.

Even though she knew she shouldn't, Dani loved this part. The confusion on the demon's face. The moment they calculate their odds of turning the situation around, of convincing a simple human they couldn't possibly be right.

But Danika was far from simple.

Confusion creased Lana's brow. She stopped dancing. Her irises flickered between demonic red and human blue. "Are you looking to make a deal?" she asked, a new kind of excitement brightening her tone.

"The only deal I'm interested in," Dani said, reaching for the small knife hidden at her back, "is one that ends with you banished back to hell."

A shock of pain exploded across Dani's jaw. Blood coated her tongue. When she blinked back the sudden burst of stars, the succubus was slipping out the back door.

"Dammit." Dani spit a mouthful of blood onto the polished wood floor, tucked the knife back in its sheath, and took off after the demon.

The Ink itched against her skin, but she couldn't release them, not in a place as crowded as Obsidian. The club was packed with humans and demons, both problematic for their own reasons. Besides, there was no way to know for sure which humans were necromancers, and Dani couldn't afford to reveal herself as the Ink Carrier.

Dani pushed through the crowd and followed

Lana out the back door. It opened to the kitchen, and Dani caught a flash of golden curls as Lana disappeared out the fire exit. None of the chefs in the kitchen seemed to mind, or even notice, the intrusion. Dani raced down the aisle, not stopping even when she saw an alarming amount of blood-filled jars on the counter.

She'd deal with whatever the hell that was later.

The metal door clanged against the brick exterior as Dani burst into the frigid night. Her breath came out white before her, and something whistled through the air. She ducked at the last second, a metal pipe slamming into the brick where her head had been a second ago.

Dani pivoted and lunged for Lana, catching the demon around the waist. The pair fell to the ground in a flurry of limbs, each trying to find purchase around the other woman's throat. Dani grappled with the succubus and managed to clamp a hand around her throat.

"Why did you have to take this body? Why?" Tears burned in Dani's eyes. Cassie's sister was already dead, and now it was up to Dani to banish the demon inside her. Dani raised her knife, ready to plunge it into Lana's heart.

"Wouldn't you like to know." The succubus lunged and bit down on Dani's wrist.

The shock of pain forced the blade from Dani's hand. She screamed, releasing the creature's neck and punching her hard across the face. On the third blow, the demon released her hold on Dani's shredded skin and backed away.

Her entire demeanor softened, and she folded in on herself. "Oh my god, I'm so sorry!" Lana stared up at Dani, blood streaking down her face. "Are you all right?"

"I . . . What?" Still on her knees, Dani gripped her wrist, desperate to stop the bleeding. If she could stem it just a little, the magic of the Ink would heal her. She stared at the woman cowering before her, at her now bright blue eyes. "Lana?"

Pain exploded on the side of her head. Dani fell sideways, clutching her bleeding face. The succubus laughed and leapt to her feet. She moved inhumanly fast, but instead of running, she grinned wickedly at Dani, her pointed teeth dripping with red.

Dani pulled herself up, her heart racing in her chest. *Kiva,* she thought. She needed Kiva.

She started to form the word on her lips, but the back door banged open. The hot guy from the bar, Raj, stumbled out, his eyes going wide when he spotted Dani and Lana.

"What's going on out here?"

Dammit. She couldn't release the Ink in front of a

necromancer, not unless she wanted to either expose her secret or kill him. And without her normal sword, just a small knife at her disposal, killing him if he attacked first wouldn't be easy.

". . . Are you bleeding?" Raj approached Dani, concern in his eyes, but he barely spared a glance for the blood-soaked succubus in the alley with him.

Big mistake.

Lana grabbed Raj's jacket and tossed him like he weighed nothing. He soared through the air and crashed head first into the metal dumpster. He fell to the ground and went deathly still.

Before Dani had time to react, the succubus sprung forward and aimed a clenched fist at Dani's face. She barely blocked the attack in time, and then a new dance began in earnest. The faint pulse of the music still threaded the air as the pair ducked and dodged and attacked.

"Of all the crooks and demon groupies in Black-thorn, you had to pick Lana," Dani said, pinning the succubus to the side of the club and kneeing the crea-ture in the gut until it doubled over. "She has a kid sister." A punch to the temple. "Someone who *needs* *her* to survive."

"Cassie . . . " The succubus fell still, all the fight leaving her body. She collapsed to her knees and tears spilled down her face. "Is Cassie okay? Is she safe?"

This demon was giving Danika whiplash. Violent one second, a whimpering mess the next.

"Why do you care? You killed her last living relative. She's all alone, thanks to *you*." Dani backed up a few paces, not about to fall for the same stunt twice. A dozen paces to her left, her blade sat against the pavement, shiny with the blood from her aching wrist. Already the skin was stitching itself back together, an irritating and rather distracting sensation.

"Cassie is all I care about." Lana followed Dani's gaze and her lower lip trembled. "Please don't hurt me. Cassie needs me. Needs both of us."

Something cold trembled inside Dani. It shouldn't be possible. "Lana? Is that you?"

Glass shattered, the sound high and bright, and then Lana crumbled to the ground.

aj stood before Dani, a broken beer bottle in one hand. "Are you all right?" He dropped the remains of his bottle and reached toward Dani. "Did she hurt you?"

"I'm fine." Dani ignored his outstretched hand and collected her knife from the ground. "What the hell were you thinking? I had things perfectly under control." She glared at the necromancer. No matter the concern or warmth in his eyes, he had just royally screwed her. She was *this close* to a breakthrough with Lana. She had never seen a human's soul come through after a possession. All of the possessions she'd seen before were demons taking over a dead body. But if Lana was able to come through, did that mean she was alive in there? Maybe there *was* a way to save Cassie's sister.

"What was I—" He let out a frustrated sigh. "I didn't want you to get killed, but next time, I'll let the demon eat you." Raj brushed the dirt from his black suit, looking affronted. "Ungrateful wannabe demon hunter," he muttered.

"Excuse me?" Dani couldn't hide her shock. She knew there were other demon hunters in the world, most of them misguided family members of humans who bargained away their lives for fame or fortune, but Dani never expected a necromancer to try to help one. And she sure as hell never expected to be mistaken for one of those amateurs.

Raj raised one of his perfectly manicured brows at her. "Don't bother denying it. Why else would you be trying to kill a succubus? Did she screw your boyfriend?"

Dani touched the side of her head where Lana had smashed it with a rock. Her fingers came away bloody, but the wound felt sealed over. "Who says I was trying to kill her?"

"If that's your idea of foreplay, you two deserve each other. Have fun when she wakes up." Raj turned to leave before Dani could explain, but he stumbled with his first step and barely managed to catch himself against the wall.

A trail of blood trickled down his neck, staining his shirt.

"You're hurt."

"Am I?" Raj reached for his head, wincing at the touch. He leaned more heavily against the wall. "Huh, I guess I am."

Without thinking, Dani crossed the small alley and reached for Raj, supporting his weight when his legs gave out beneath him. She lowered him gently to the ground and checked the wound on his scalp. Poe's energy burned hot against her skin, but even though she knew she didn't have time for this, knew that Raj was supposed to be her enemy, her instincts shouted at her to help.

"Is there someplace quiet I can patch you up? This needs to be cleaned before it gets infected." Dani glanced at Lana's still form. If Cassie's big sister was somewhere locked inside, if those flashes of humanity were real and not a trick to lower Dani's defenses, then she'd need a private place to question the demon and find a way to save Lana.

Raj tried to wave her off. "I'm fine."

"You're not fine," Dani insisted, brushing the fallen strands of hair out of his face. His skin was hot against hers, and his closeness stirred something inside Dani. She felt herself soften toward him, even as Poe grew more irritated against her chest. "Let me help you."

A series of conflicting emotions flickered across

Raj's face. "What about her?" He gestured weakly toward Lana.

"She's my friend's sister. Or, she was, anyway. I'm hoping there's something I can do to save her." Dani bit her lip, glancing at the injured necromancer. "I don't suppose you could help with that?"

Raj was silent a moment, reaching up to feel the wound on his head. He winced and reached out for Dani, leaning on her to get to his feet. "I don't know if I can help, but I live a few blocks away. If you can stop the bleeding, I'll let you use my place to deal with your friend."

"Really?" Dani cautiously followed Raj as he moved unsteadily down the alley.

"Seems like a fair enough trade to me." He reached into his pocket and pulled out a set of keys. "My car is parked around the corner."

"You drove here when you only live a few blocks away?"

A teasing smile tugged at his lips. "You never know when you might get jumped by a succubus in the back alley."

"Fair enough." Dani stooped and picked up Lana, half-dragging, half-carrying her down the alley and around the corner. Despite her enhanced strength, she was glad to see Raj's car was indeed right there. He popped the trunk and helped her settle the demon inside. But when he went for the driver's seat, Dani grabbed hold of his wrist. "I'm not letting you drive with a possible concussion. Besides, you've also been drinking." She reached for the keys.

"I'm fine." Raj held out his arms and touched his fingers to his nose and back again, performing an impromptu field sobriety test. "See?"

Dani swiped the keys from his palm and let them dangle in front of his face. "If you can't hold onto your keys, you can't drive." She unlocked the car and led him around to the passenger side, putting one hand on her hip and staring him down until he climbed into the car.

She slammed his door shut and let out a shaky breath as she crossed to the driver's seat. Poe would give her the lecture of a lifetime if he found out she went anywhere near a necromancer without one of the Ink already out for backup, yet here she was, driving one home with a succubus in the trunk.

Raj directed Dani through the downtown streets and into a swanky neighborhood, where he led her to one of the biggest houses she'd ever seen. "You seriously live here?"

"For a couple years now. I moved out of my dad's place when I turned eighteen." He pressed a button above the dash and the garage door lifted soundlessly.

The garage was bigger than Dani's last three

apartments combined. A surge of anger flickered as she pulled in. It wasn't fair. Her sacred duty, to 'rid the world of evil' as Poe often put it, left her so broke she could barely keep a roof over her head, while necromancers—the bringers of said evil—had more wealth than they could ever possibly use.

Dani shoved the jealousy down long enough to park the car and grab the still unconscious demon from the trunk. She followed Raj inside the house, where she was rendered speechless. Soaring high ceilings were finished with polished wood accents. Marble floors stretched across the main level. Sweeping double staircases led to the second floor and reminded Dani of a fairytale. Everything was so big and open and *bright*.

"Can I get you a drink?" Raj asked once they'd settled Lana into a chair in the foyer.

"You can bring me rope and a first aid kit." She stood and rubbed her wrist, where her own skin had stitched fully shut. "And *you* should not be drinking with a head injury."

Raj held his hands in surrender and disappeared somewhere in the massive home. Dani wanted to call to him, if only to see if the sound would echo back at her. She didn't get a chance before Raj returned with the supplies in hand. She bound Lana to the chair and tested the knots. They held firm.

She wished she could leave one of the Ink to stand guard over Lana, but Dani didn't want Raj to know who she truly was. Still, leaving a demon with nothing but rope to bind them wasn't exactly ideal. "I don't suppose you have any sort of magic that'll keep our guest contained?"

"I've never had cause to try." But Raj raised his hands anyway and sketched sigils in the air. His arms shook—whether from effort or his injuries, Dani couldn't tell—but the air shimmered with power.

"That'll work?" Dani asked, unsure if he had done enough to keep Lana in place if she managed to uncoil the knots.

Raj shrugged. "They're meant to be shields, and they can only take so much damage without rein-forcement, but they'll slow her down at least."

It would have to be good enough, at least until Dani finished with her part of the bargain. She tried not to act too impressed with his magic. Though this was the first time she'd seen this kind of power in action, she knew necromancers like Raj only gained their abilities through demonic deals. "How do you want to do this?"

Confusion settled over Raj's features until Dani picked up the first aid kit. "Oh. Right. The kitchen is probably the best spot." He led Dani through the house. They passed huge works of art secured in intricate golden frames, a living room with the largest TV Dani had ever seen, and finally stepped into the kitchen.

"Are you sure I can't get you a drink?" Raj asked as he sat in one of the high stools at the granite island.

"Positive." Dani took the first aid kit and spread it out along the counter. She wet the incredibly soft paper towels in the sink and started her work by wiping away the blood on Raj's face and neck. He winced as she got near the wound itself. "Sorry," she muttered, lightening her touch.

"No, it's fine." Raj smiled, but it was a strained thing. "I'm being a baby. You're surprisingly gentle for someone who held their own against a demon." Warmth spread inside Dani at his words, but she didn't say anything. Raj considered her with open interest. "What exactly were you doing at Obsidian?"

Dani paused, her hand poised to wipe the last of the blood from Raj's face. She could play coy and try to dodge the question, but she was on Raj's turf. There was no reason to guess he'd give up on asking. "My friend's sister went missing. She had a card with Obsidian's name and address on it. I went there to find her."

"And the sister is . . . "

"The succubus currently tied up in your house? Yup." Dani reached for a bottle of disinfectant. "Hold still. This might sting." She poured disinfectant over the wound, using the paper towel to catch the extra liquid as it slid down his face.

Raj grit his teeth and fell silent while Dani continued her work, drying and dressing the wound. She secured the bandage, her fingers pressing lightly against Raj's clean skin. When she stepped back to examine her work, Raj reached for her hand.

"Thank you." His skin was like fire against hers, and something stirred inside Dani's chest.

She forced herself to pull away from his touch. "Don't mention it." It was suddenly way too hot in the house. Dani slipped off her leather jacket, draping it over another stool, and washed her hands in the sink.

"Nice tattoos."

Dani froze, the water still running over her hands. She glanced up at Raj, searching his face for any sign that he realized who she really was. But he smiled at her, a warm, non-threatening thing. She shut off the water and dried her hands on a fresh paper towel. "What were *you* doing at Obsidian tonight?" she asked, changing the subject.

Raj shrugged. "I'm there most nights. I own the place."

A sick feeling settled in Dani's gut. How had she missed it? "You're a *Dasari?*" Then she realized, with sickening clarity, what his full name must be. "*Rajan*

Dasari?" Raj wasn't just some flirty necromancer, he was the sole heir to the Dasari empire. And if the rumors about his father's health troubles were true, he'd be more than an heir before the year was out.

Poe was going to peck her eyes out for this. She should have left Raj to his injuries. His family made their fortune brokering deals with demons; she shouldn't be tending to him like some wannabe nurse. And she sure as hell shouldn't notice how damn attractive he was.

But Raj only grimaced. "No one calls me Rajan except my father. Raj is fine."

Dani almost laughed at the absurdity of it. As if his preference for a nickname was at all the point she was trying to make.

"My, my, aren't you two quite the pair." A sultry voice slipped into the room with them.

Dani and Raj turned . . .

And found Lana standing in the archway.

The succubus leaned against the wall and traced her finger tips up and down her exposed chest, raising little goosebumps on Lana's skin. "I could get a contact high off the tension in this room."

Dani's face burned, and she couldn't bring herself to look at Raj. She grabbed a knife from the block on the counter. "You'll stay right there if you value your time on earth."

"Oh relax, little hunter. I'm not looking for a fight." The succubus sidled up to Raj, her hips swaying with each step, and draped one arm over his shoulders. "Playing is so much more fun," she whispered, her lips brushing against his golden-brown skin. "And it's been a minute since I've been with two lovers at once."

"Not interested." Dani raised the knife. "Back off, demon."

"Pity." The succubus pulled away from Raj, letting her fingers trail across his shoulders. "This body is so very alive. It would be such fun." In a flash, the demon grabbed the back of Raj's stool, dragged it halfway across the room, and settled herself in his lap.

"Fucking succubi," Dani grumbled as Lana pressed her lips against Raj's neck and writhed in his lap.

The necromancer shot her a worried look. He should be able to hold his own against a demon, but either this succubus was especially strong or the combination of alcohol and head trauma had lowered his usual defenses. Soon, his expression melted into a dazed hunger, and he reached for Lana, settling his hands on the small of her back.

"You've made your point, demon. That's enough."

Lana ignored her, bringing her hands to rest on either side of Raj's neck. She kissed him fiercely, and his body responded to her touch, pulling her closer. When the succubus pulled away, the air shimmered bright with Raj's essence, and Lana breathed it in.

Raj shuddered, and a sickly sheen coated his face.

"Get the hell off him," Dani snapped. She grabbed Lana by the upper arm to pull her away, but the demon twisted suddenly, her elbow smashing into

Dani's nose. The burst of pain sent her stumbling back.

"Wait your turn, hunter," the succubus snapped, drawing another lungful of Raj's energy into her being. His hands fell limp at his sides.

Dani cursed under her breath and wiped away the blood dripping down her face. She was way too tired —and too damn hungry—to deal with this nonsense a second longer. "Silas!"

Her right arm burned as Silas stripped himself from her skin, slinking to the floor. When his body was fully corporeal, the python glanced up at his Carrier. Dani gestured at the moaning succubus, who was reaching for the buttons on Raj's shirt.

Silas slipped silently across the marble floor, his black scales shimmering in the bright lights. He climbed up the stool and wrapped himself around Lana's torso, hissing in her face, a fierce, soul-shuddering sound. Lana froze. Her head whipped around until she found Dani, her eyes wide with fear.

"Off. Now." Dani commanded, and the succubus complied. She slipped from Raj's lap as Silas tightened across her chest, pinning her arms to her side. "Sit." Dani kicked a chair toward the succubus.

"You'll pay for this," Lana growled, but she obeyed.

"I'm sure," Dani said, rubbing the bare spot on her forearm. Now that she had one of the Ink on her side, she wasn't afraid of the demon's taunts, even if using her Ink presented other challenges. She cast a glance at Raj, who looked extremely uncomfortable as he crossed his legs and straightened out his shirt. "You good, Romeo?"

The necromancer scrubbed his face and looked between Silas and Dani. "Am I hallucinating? Where'd the giant snake come from?"

Dani shifted uncomfortably, but the succubus just laughed. "You don't recognize the Ink Carrier? You tasted smarter than that."

Recognition lit Raj's features, slowly at first, smoothing out the confused lines on his forehead, until suddenly he snapped his clear eyes in Dani's direction. "The tattoos. You're—"

"Tired of this conversation," Dani cut in, shielding her now bare arm from Raj's view. There really wasn't a point in trying to hide the truth; he clearly already knew enough to be a danger to her, but she couldn't quell the instinct.

"But you're so young," Raj said, pressing the issue. "I've heard stories of the Ink Carrier my whole life. My grandfather dealt with the Carrier, too."

"Probably *my* grandmother," Dani conceded in the hopes that with some answers, Raj would move on. Though in truth, it might have been her great-grandmother. The Frost women had children young and didn't live long lives. "Can we focus? I have a soul to save."

Dani approached the succubus, who had given up on trying to escape Silas's hold. For once, the demon actually looked scared, which hopefully meant she'd be willing to cooperate.

"You know who I am," Dani said simply, "which means you know what will happen if you piss me off. Silas can send you back to your demonic realm with a single bite."

As if to confirm Dani's false threat—the snakes needed to consume demons completely to send them back—Silas flicked his tongue against Lana's neck. The demon flinched.

"Let's start with your name."

"I'd rather claw my way back to hell than give you my true name."

All demons had a thing about names. Names held power, and knowing their true name gave the person who spoke it complete control over them.

Dani sighed. She was already exhausted by the creature and they'd only just begun. "I don't need your true name. What do you like to be called in this realm?"

The succubus glanced nervously from Dani to Raj. "It's Pam."

"Pam. Seriously?" Dani had expected something like Veronica or Jezebel. Not *Pam.*

She nodded. "What's wrong with Pam? I like it."

"Fine, *Pam.* I believe Lana is still alive, shoved back somewhere in that sick head of yours. I need to speak with her."

"Why?" Pam whined, drawing out the word. "She's not nearly as fun as me. *Completely* boring in bed." The demon looked past Dani, to where Raj was finally getting to his feet. "If you let me go, I can make you forget all about Lana. *And* your little bodyguard." At that last bit, Pam jerked her head toward Dani before returning her smoldering gaze on Raj. She licked her lips seductively, until Silas hissed and snapped his mighty jaws in her face.

Raj stepped forward until he was even with Dani. He crossed his arms against his chest, and Dani couldn't help but notice the way his tight shirt showed off every curve of his muscles. "Enough games. Let the girl through before I find the necromancer who raised you and make them send you back. No snake bites required." At that, he glanced at Dani, but she couldn't read his expression. He should hate her, but that wasn't the emotion written in his eyes. Even so, she couldn't imagine he liked having the Ink Carrier at his house.

But then why is he helping me?

"Fine," Pam said, pulling Dani back to the moment. "But don't say I didn't warn you. If you all die of boredom, that's not on me." The succubus tilted her head back and shuddered, an exaggerated moan falling off her lips, until finally she fell still.

"Lana?" Dani cautiously stepped toward the bound demon. "Lana, can you hear me?"

Another moan—this one less sexual, more the sound of someone waking up with a terrible hangover—and then Lana's head tipped back up. Fear permeated her gaze when it focused on Dani. But then she glanced down at the snake around her body and screamed.

"It's okay! Just relax," Dani said, rushing forward. "Silas, return."

Of course, his voice hissed in her mind as he burst into a cloud of ink and etched himself back onto her skin.

Dani did her best to hide the pain from Raj, who watched closely as the python etched back into her skin. When it was done, she focused her attention on Lana. "See, the giant snake is gone. You're okay." Dani knelt beside the still sitting woman. "Do you know who you are? Do you remember what . . . " She trailed off, not sure how much of the possession to mention in case Lana didn't recall a thing.

"You have to bring it back. You can't get rid of the

demon." Tears spilled down Lana's face, but her expression was fierce. "Please tell me you didn't banish her. Please!"

That was not at all the reaction Dani expected. At worst she was expecting confusion and a totally blank memory. Hell, maybe even some gratitude for giving her soul control of her body again. Not this angry panic. And she sure as hell didn't expect Lana to *want* the demon.

"Hey there, it's okay." Raj's voice was soothing where Dani's had gone silent. "Let me get you something to drink. I've got whiskey, wine, probably a couple beers in the fridge."

"Water's fine," Lana said, one hand coming to rest at her throat. "Pam forgets I need something other than alcohol to drink."

"Wait. Everybody . . . just . . . wait. You *know* the succubus? You're okay with being possessed?" Dani stood and ran a hand over her face. *What the hell is the world coming to?* "I need you to back up and explain."

Lana glared at her. "Why should I explain anything to *you?*"

"Because your sister Cassie is scared out of her mind and all alone," Dani snapped, causing the little color left in Lana's cheeks to fade away.

"You spoke to Cassie?"

"Yes, I did. She's been canvassing the city looking

for you. She's a *child,* Lana. She needs someone home to look after her." Dani wanted to scream, but when Raj returned with a glass of water, she forced herself to take a deep breath. "Please, Lana. Help me understand what's going on here."

"I did what any parent would do." Lana paused and downed the entire glass of water, her hands trembling and her eyes filling with tears. "My baby sister was dying. Do you have any idea how hard that was to watch? She's so *young.* She was wasting away."

"That's why you came to Obsidian," Raj cut in, but Lana shook her head.

"Not at first. We tried everything we could afford. Chemo. Radiation. Acupuncture. Special herbal teas. Reiki. I tried *everything* to save my sister, but nothing worked. And then . . . And then Cassie gave up." Lana's voice broke and she buried her face in her hands.

Dani remembered the calendar full of notes, the little red X's that crossed out all the upcoming appointments. "Cassie didn't want to be too sick from treatments to enjoy the last days of her life."

Lana scowled. "She's a *child.* She shouldn't get to decide."

"But that's what finally sent you to Obsidian," Dani guessed.

"I'd heard rumors around town, that you could

find miracles at Obsidian. I cashed out everything we had left from our parents' life insurance policies, took out a second mortgage on the house, and went searching for a cure." Lana glanced down, rubbing one finger along the edge of the glass. "I found a man at the club. He said if I agreed to share my body with a demon, it would remove Cassie's cancer."

"And did it?" Dani asked. The Cassie she'd met still looked frail, but even with the cancer itself cured, it would take time for her body to heal.

"It did. I forced her to go to her check-up appointment, and Cassie's doctors called a few days later to say the cancer was gone. They couldn't believe it. They wanted to run more tests to make sure it wasn't an error at the lab, but I knew it had worked. My baby sister was safe."

Tears spilled down Lana's cheeks, the relief of the news still clearly overwhelming. But then she blinked, and a scowl creased her brow. "I never even got a chance to tell Cassie the good news. As soon as her cancer was gone, Pam took over completely. She wouldn't let me out anymore. I was supposed to keep the daylight hours to take care of Cassie, but she took that from me, too."

"This necromancer," Raj cut in, his voice sharp, "who was he?"

Lana shook her head. "He never gave his name.

Just took the money and led me to a back room, where he summoned the demon and made the deal."

"Is there anything you remember?" Raj pushed, growing more agitated. "A tattoo or special marking or anything?"

"I don't know. He was some tall white guy with a bald head and a beard."

"There has to be more than that," Raj pressed, almost aggressively.

"What's wrong with you?" Dani asked, staring daggers at him. She cared far less about which necromancer brokered the deal than how to banish the demon back to hell.

Her questions seemed to dislodge whatever anger had Raj's hands curled into fists. He reached for the bottle of whiskey on the cabinet. "The club didn't sanction this deal. I'm supposed to get fifteen percent." He tossed back a shot of the amber liquid. "When I find out who did this, I'm banning him from Obsidian. And collecting interest."

Raj took another shot, but Dani watched him curiously. Something about his demeanor said this was about more than an issue of lost income. But why would he care? He probably brokered the same sorts of deals all the time.

Dani shuddered at the thought of Raj in some dark room, raising up demons and binding their monstrous souls to recent corpses. But she didn't have time to ponder the politics of necromancers. She turned back to Lana. "It's going to be okay. We'll find a way to banish Pam and get your life back."

"No!" Lana shot up from the chair. "You can't."

"Don't worry," Dani soothed, "It won't hurt."

"I don't care about that." Lana scrubbed the lingering tears from her cheeks, her expression fierce. "If you send the demon away, Cassie's cancer will come back. She'll die. You have to leave things the way they are."

"I'm sorry, Lana, but I can't do that." Dani glanced back at Raj, who was watching her with open interest. "I can't let the succubus roam the world unchecked. She's dangerous."

"You'd rather condemn my baby sister to death?" Lana's voice rose with each word until they landed against Dani like blows. "Pam doesn't even kill anyone! I can see everything she does. At worst, she breaks up a few already rocky marriages. What does that matter when the alternative is losing Cassie?"

Dani didn't like the thought of Cassie's death any more than her sister did, but she couldn't let Pam keep control of Lana's body. Especially with Lana still alive. If her effect on Raj was any indication, a living body made Pam's powers all the more powerful. Lana was only willing to bear the cost to save her sister's life, but she couldn't even watch out for Cassie the way things were. Her sister was basically an orphan.

"Silas. Jasper." Dani winced as both snakes peeled from her skin. "Watch her," she said, pointing to Lana. "Don't let her out of your sight."

Can we bite her? Jasper asked. *Can we eat her?*

"No, you can't eat her," Dani replied, which made Lana startle as the python and king cobra circled her. "Poe?" She wasn't thrilled about giving him the chance to lecture at her, but she was running out of ideas.

The raven burst from her chest with more speed and ferocity than she'd ever experienced before. The power of it left her breathless, and Poe sprung into the air and dove at Raj, talons reaching for his face.

"Poe, wait! We're not under attack."

But she was too late. The bird dove at Raj, who ducked at the last second, grabbing a lid from the drying rack by the sink to use as a shield.

"Dammit, Poe," she yelled when he circled again. "Stop or I'll return you."

This boy is the enemy, Danika. Where's your sword? You should run him through. Poe landed on the fridge and loosed an indignant squawk.

Dani groaned. "The both of you, in the next room. Now."

Raj didn't release his culinary shield, but he

followed her into a living room. Dani quickly explained the situation to Poe. "There has to be a way to get rid of the succubus without reversing Cassie's cure."

Poe shook his head, the movement ruffling his feathers. *The terms of the ill-advised agreement seem clear enough. The cancer only stays gone as long as the demon is inside the elder sister's body.*

"So, what do we do?" Dani asked, desperate for a solution, while Raj watched her with growing confusion, unable to hear Poe's words.

We send the demon back. I'll teach you how.

"But—"

No 'buts,' Danika. The deal should not have been made in the first place. Poe hopped closer and nuzzled his head into her shoulder. *I know it's sad, but the girl would have died anyway. This will simply set the world back the way it should be.*

"That's not good enough," Dani snapped, drawing away from the bird. "There has to be a way to keep the demon *here* but keep it contained in some way."

"Actually," Raj interrupted, still keeping a wary eye on Poe. "I might know someone who could help with that."

Dani sat in the passenger seat of Raj's car, the leather soft beneath her, and watched the necromancer as he drove north. Something about the set of his features, the focus pulling at his brow, made her question everything she'd learned ever about necromancers. They were all supposed to be the same. Ruthless. Incapable of empathy. Power hungry to a fault.

Rajan Dasari didn't appear to be any of those things, and Dani couldn't reconcile that fact against everything she'd learned. Perhaps she'd missed too much training. Perhaps there was more nuance to necromancers that her mother hadn't had the chance to teach her. Or perhaps some were better at hiding the ways their demonic dealings affected them.

The heir to the Dasari empire glanced at Dani, catching her staring. "Is everything all right?"

"Yeah. Fine. Why wouldn't it be?"

"One, I can tell you're lying. And two, you're rubbing your arms. Does it hurt to be this far from your. . . " He fumbled for the right word. "Your snakes?"

Dani's hands stilled on her forearms. She hadn't noticed the nervous motion. "They're called the Ink, and no, it doesn't hurt." She shouldn't be telling him any of this. It was too dangerous for the necromancers to know anything about her. She was the last of her kind, and the world couldn't afford for her enemies to have any advantage.

It sounded extreme, hyperbolic even, but it wasn't. She was the only thing standing between demons and their full control of the mortal realm. Sure, sometimes humans who had close encounters with demons became self-proclaimed hunters, but they took down so few demons—and got killed often enough themselves—that they barely even tipped the scale.

"I don't understand you," Dani said at last, turning the conversation away from her many secrets. "Why are you helping me?"

"You did patch up my head."

"I'm sure you say that to all the demon hunters."

Raj laughed, but the sound quickly died in his throat. The energy in the car shifted, grew serious. They rolled to a stop before a red light, and Raj used the momentary stillness to look at Dani. Everything inside shouted at her to look away. She didn't. "I can guess what you think of people like me," he started, "but most of us are born to this. We don't choose this life."

"You're an adult. Make another choice."

"You try telling a father like mine that you don't want to follow in his footsteps." Raj shook his head and stepped hard on the gas when the light turned green. "I might as well tell him I want to marry a white girl."

Dani raised an eyebrow.

"Indian fathers have a very specific blueprint for their sons. Necromancers doubly so."

"Are you scared of him?"

Raj shook his head. "No, it's not— Never mind. I don't think it's the kind of thing you could understand. Let's just say there's no disobeying Hasan Dasari."

Dani nodded, though she bristled at the idea that she wouldn't understand. If he took the time to explain, she thought she would. "You never answered my question."

"Didn't I?" Raj took a sharp left, the tires squealing

against the pavement. He didn't elaborate as he parallel parked along the street, nestling his monstrosity of a car beside other vehicles that cost more than Dani would make in five years. He cut the engine and reached for the door handle.

"Raj, wait." Dani grabbed his arm, and as her fingers wrapped around his skin, something warm bloomed in her chest. She let go, but he was already turning back to look at her, releasing the door. Through the window, Dani could see the party spilling out of the mansion, and the bass from the stereo was already shaking the car. "You can't honestly expect me to waltz in there, no questions asked."

"No one said waltzing was a requirement."

"Raj."

"I know. I'm sorry." He leaned back against his head rest, and he suddenly looked much younger than Dani first thought, probably closer to twenty than twenty-five. "If I have to be what I am," he said, side-stepping the word *necromancer*, "I need lines I won't cross. Something to keep whatever might be left of my soul intact. And I swore when I took over the club that I'd enforce that line."

He paused, running a hand through his long hair, wincing when his fingers brushed too close to his injury. "Everyone who makes a deal in Obsidian is supposed to fully understand what they're giving up. That's my line. I will not condemn a soul without their informed consent, and I certainly wouldn't permit this kind of living possession."

Dani smiled. "You sound like a doctor. Some demonic version of 'do no harm'."

A flicker of warmth curved the corner of Raj's lips, but it disappeared before it could blossom into anything more. "That woman you're helping, she was tricked into making a deal before she fully understood the implications. I can't let that happen in my club without consequences."

"She might have made the same choice, even if she had known." In the few moments of talking to the real Lana, Dani could tell the woman would do *anything* to save her sister.

Raj looked at Dani then, a gaze so penetrating and raw that she struggled not to flinch away. "This is the only way I can reduce the harm of what I am, Danika. I won't tell anyone who you are. I'll make sure we help Lana and her little sister." He reached out a hand, like he meant to hold hers, but diverted at the last second and rested his fingers against the gear shift instead. "Do you trust me?"

Dani swallowed, her mouth suddenly too dry to speak. She felt as though she held Raj's battered heart in her hands. It fluttered wildly, a skittish thing ready to bolt. She nodded.

"Right then." Raj swung out of the car, leaving Dani scrambling after him. "Let's see a man about a demon."

Inside the house, the party raged so fiercely, it overloaded every one of Dani's enhanced senses. The music's heavy drums and pounding bass crushed her thoughts out of her head. The flashing lights and bodies covered with neon paint flooded her vision. Incense, sweat, and more than a little marijuana permeated the air until it was hard to breathe.

Dani hated every bit of the overload. She wanted to run. She would have if not for Raj's steadying hand against the small of her back. His voice, smooth and sultry, was the only thing she could make out above the noise. He told her the house belonged to a childhood friend of his, the man most likely to know how to help Lana. Someone who'd be willing to provide said help to a hunter like Dani.

They searched the perimeter of the house first, checking the kitchen, patio, and even the billiard room. When they'd covered the entire house except for the crush of bodies that had transformed the grand entrance and dining room into a giant dance hall, they were left with no other choice but to dive into the fray.

Partygoers shot them dagger-sharp looks as they tried to push their way through. Dani's already overloaded senses threatened to drown her. With so many sweaty bodies pressing against her, so many glancing touches, she wanted to disappear. To scream. When another highly intoxicated man jostled into Dani, her hands curled into fists. Before she could strike the man down, strong arms looped around her stomach and pressed her tight against a firm chest.

"Breathe, Dani." Raj's voice hovered at her ear, worming in despite music that shook every cell inside her body. "These are all humans," he said, moving them through the crowd in time with the music, blocking her body from wayward arms and jostling dancers. "I don't think you want to hit them."

"I wasn't going to hit him," she grumbled.

"Liar," he said, but his body started to move in beat with the music. "We should probably dance. We don't want to attract suspicion while we look for my friend."

A shiver traveled down her spine, and her body melted into Raj. She wanted to dance with him. Wanted to forget about all her responsibilities and let herself get lost in the thrum of music and the steady presence of Raj pressed against her.

Before Dani could say anything, Raj went still, his laugh tickling against her ear. "Never mind. There's Spencer." He raised a hand to point.

Dani followed the path to a pair of men dancing near the center of the room. They were both undeniably handsome and completely lost in each other. The white man with a shock of deep blue curls turned to face the tall Latino dancing behind him. Their fingers twined together, and the shorter man accepted a kiss that was far from chaste.

Even though she'd witnessed a succubus grind all over Raj, something about the connection between these men made her cheeks flush. There was something so real about their connection, something the demon could never recreate. She pulled away from Raj's touch, which suddenly felt far too intimate for their precarious alliance. "Which one's Spencer?"

Raj ignored her and approached the dancing men. "Spence!" he shouted, his voice barely carrying over the music.

The blue-haired man glanced over his shoulder, though Dani couldn't imagine how he'd heard his name called over the noise. His eyes were glassy and unfocused, but when he saw Raj, the widest grin split his face.

"Raj!" The man flung himself at the necromancer, hugging him tight. "What are you doing here? Who's this?" He sized up Dani as she approached.

"Can we talk in private?" Raj glanced behind Spencer, where his date was slowly coming toward them.

"Of course." Spencer reached for his dance partner's hand. "You remember Adrian, don't you?"

Raj smiled. "Nice to see you again."

Adrian raised Spencer's hand to his lips and pressed a kiss to his knuckles. "I assume Raj is going to steal you away for the night?" The man sounded disappointed but unsurprised.

"Hopefully not too long," Spencer said, casting an assessing look at Dani. "I'll come find you when we're finished."

The man nodded and disappeared into the crush of dancing bodies.

Spencer watched him go, something soft in his eyes, before nodding for Raj and Dani to follow. He led them upstairs into a linen closet, where he pressed on the back of the shelving and the whole wall swung out, exposing another set of stairs. Dani got the distinct impression that she could be killed in this secret floor and no one would ever find her body, but she forced herself to follow anyway.

If things went sideways, she still had Kiva and Poe on her side.

The stairwell gave way to a large room. Shelves lined the walls and were filled to bursting with leather-bound books, clear glass jars of varying sizes, and neatly arranged wooden boxes. A large work table sat at the center of the room with beakers and hotplates. The whole room had the feel of a chemist's lab, and it was neater than Dani would have guessed, given the rave happening downstairs.

When the door closed behind them, blocking out the last of the music, Spencer finally turned to face Dani and Raj. The fun party boy disappeared completely, leaving behind a young man with sharp, inquisitive eyes and the beginnings of a frown. "What's wrong?"

Raj looked affronted. "Why does something have to be wrong?"

"Really?" Spencer cocked his head to one side and gave them both an apprising look. "You show up at one of my parties, with a girl I've never seen before, and need to speak in private? If that isn't code for Raj-Is-In-Trouble, I don't know what is."

Before Raj could try to deny Spencer's claim, Dani jumped in. "Who are you, exactly? And how many times has Raj played the damsel in distress?"

Spencer laughed, a full-bodied sound that filled

the entirety of his secret lab. "I'm Spencer Owens," he said, extending a hand. "Always a pleasure to meet someone who gives Raj a hard time."

"Owens?" Dani asked, her warmth toward Spencer freezing over. "As in the Owens family of necromancers?" While not the most powerful of the five families, Poe had warned that the Owens clan was the most radical. They worshipped demons as gods and were willing to sacrifice anything to appease their twisted deities, which made them dangerously unpredictable.

But Spencer only sighed. "Unfortunately." He crossed the room and leaned against the work table, completely at ease among his beakers and tinctures. "If it makes you feel any better, I've been thoroughly disowned by my family."

Dani softened toward him, but only slightly. "Why?"

"It's a long story, but suffice it to say they didn't appreciate it when I fell in love with Adrian instead of agreeing to join their demonic priesthood."

"I believe your 'heretical views of your demon masters' was another of your father's common refrains," Raj added, and Dani couldn't help but wonder why Raj felt so stuck when Spencer seemed to have escaped without too much trouble.

"And what views are those?" Dani asked, slipping

out of her leather jacket. The top floor of the house was getting too warm for comfort.

Spencer's eyes grew wide when he spotted the edge of Poe's tattoo near the lowered neckline of her shirt, and a silent conversation seemed to pass between the necromancers. "Views I'm sure are not unlike your own, Ink Carrier." Spencer watched for her reaction, but she gave him none. "Do you have a name, or do you answer to Carrier?"

"It's Danika Frost. Most people call me Dani." She glanced at Raj. "He thinks you can help me." Though she didn't know if she could trust either of these men, Dani explained their predicament as succinctly as she could.

Before she even finished her explanation, Spencer had started picking through his lab, grabbing items from his shelves and arranging them on the table.

"Can you help us?" Dani asked when she finished.

Spencer started the burner on his table and set a wide-mouthed glass jar over the flame. "Yes and no," he said, grabbing a pair of safety goggles and poured a clear gelatinous substance into the jar. He muttered to himself as he ran calculations and measured out ingredients.

When he still hadn't spoken after several minutes of focused work, Dani cleared her throat. "Could you be slightly less vague?"

"Huh?" Spencer glanced up, like he's forgotten they were there. "Oh, sorry. Just . . . one sec." He continued his calculations and added a drop of something black to the mixture. There was a flash of light, and then Spencer lifted the safety goggles from his face. "Sorry, you have to time the base mixture just right or else it spoils. Now, where were we?"

"Can you help or not?"

"Right." Spencer pressed his hands into his lower back, stretching. "There's no way to banish the succubus without undoing the pact. If you kill Pam, you kill Cassie."

Dani deflated, her heart plummeting to her toes. "So that's it then? They both have to die?" She didn't think she could do it. Even though it was her job, even though generation after generation of Frost women had fought and died to eliminate demons from this world, Dani couldn't stomach the thought of Cassie dying on her watch.

"He's not done," Raj whispered, coming to stand beside Dani.

"You could kill the demon," Spencer agreed. "Or, with a little help from yours truly, you could trap the demon in the back of Lana's mind, where she wouldn't even notice Pam's influence."

"How?" A flicker of hope ignited inside Dani. She

could actually pull this off. She could save Cassie's sister, just like she promised.

Spencer lifted a gold piece from the table. "I can make an amulet that will suppress the succubus, leaving Lana to live her life as if she wasn't possessed."

"Sounds perfect," Dani said. *Too perfect.* "What's the catch?"

"No catch. The only tricky part is in the making of the amulet." He turned his attention to Raj. "I need the blood of the necromancer who performed the summoning."

Raj and Dani shared a look. "We don't know who it was," Raj admitted.

"Lana couldn't remember much about him, just that he was some tall white guy with a beard."

"That doesn't do us much good," Spencer mused, which felt like the most crushing understatement Dani had ever heard. "It obviously wasn't a Dasari, right, Raj? They wouldn't operate in your club without your approval."

"Not unless they talked to Hasan, but Dad hasn't been meeting with anyone lately. He doesn't want anyone to know about his . . . condition."

Dani noted the pained tone in Raj's voice, noted the sympathetic look Spencer gave him, but Raj didn't elaborate, and she didn't have the heart to tell him that his father's *condition* wasn't as secret as the older man hoped.

"The Conrads and Riveras are too uppity to set foot in a nightclub," Spencer added, referring to the necromancer families who had infiltrated the upper spheres of human society. The Conrads were respected politicians—well, as respected as politicians could be anyway—while the Rivera clan ran much of the business sector.

"You think a Brennan was dealing in my club?" Raj scowled, and Dani noted the change in his demeanor with interest. The rumors must be true. Despite what should be a symbiotic relationship, the Dasari family controlling the club business while the Brennans ran most of the drugs in town, the families seemed at odds.

Dani stored the tidbit of intel away, along with the other insights into Raj's world. If she intended to stay in Blackthorn and clear out the infestation of demons, pieces of information like feuds between the necromancer families was bound to come in handy at some point.

"Could be. Although I wouldn't put it past my family either." Spencer ran a hand through his hair, and the deep blue locks turned a vivid purple. "My parents blame Raj for leading me astray, so they're always looking for ways to undermine his legacy," he clarified for Dani.

Raj snorted, an irritated, petty sound. "I'm not the one who turned his back on the magic of our families. That was all you."

"Yes, but you were my only non-relative friend. They had to blame *someone* for my fall from grace. It couldn't *possibly* be their horrendous parenting skills." Spencer rolled his eyes, and Dani found herself liking him so much more than she expected. "Did Lana say anything about the summoning itself? Was it pleading or demanding?"

"She didn't say."

"Could you ask?" Spencer pointed at Dani's bare arms. "I assume you have Ink watching over her?"

How does he know I can speak with them? But there was no point denying it. He wasn't asking if it was possible, he already knew. "Give me a minute."

Dani walked away from the pair of necromancers, reaching for the thin thread of consciousness that connected her to Silas and Jasper. She tugged on the tether once she found it, and it was Silas who answered first.

Yes? His voice hissed in her head, so much quieter than if he were beside her but still crystal clear.

I need to speak with Lana. Dani closed her eyes and braced her hand against the wall as Silas's vision exploded inside her head, running like a movie reel. It was disorienting every time, the way his vision swayed as he moved.

Cassie's sister sat on the couch, Jasper curled around her feet, holding her tight. Silas slipped up the couch and across the back, coming to rest across her shoulders. Dani's body rocked and shuddered as Lana flinched under the weight of Silas.

"I need to know everything you remember about the summoning," she said, hearing an echo of her own words as Silas pushed the thoughts into Lana's mind.

"Dani? Is that you?" She looked around wildly, trying to shake Silas off her shoulder. The rocking of his vision made Dani's stomach clench.

"Focus, Lana. I can't keep this up forever."

Lana's head dropped back on the edge of the couch. After a moment, she sat up again, a seductive smile curling her lips. "Forget her," she said, her voice low and smooth. "*I* remember plenty."

"Pam," Dani said through gritted teeth. "Let Lana back through."

"No. Wait." Spencer crossed the room to where Dani was leaning against the wall for support. "The demon probably remembers more. Find out what she knows."

Dani nodded and focused on her connection with Silas, feeling his sturdy strength flow through her. "Tell me what you remember of the man who raised you, and I'll let you stay surfaced until I get back."

"Only if I get to play with Raj again."

Silas wrapped his thick body tight around Pam's torso, channeling Dani's sudden anger.

"Fine, fine!" Pam wheezed, and Silas loosened his grip. "He was handsome, with a rugged scar on the back of his neck. He said I was the most beautiful goddess he'd ever seen and promised to serve me however I saw fit." Pam smiled, as if lost in the memory, but then she stuck out her lower lip and pouted. "He was such a prude though. He wouldn't even kiss me."

A biting, sarcastic retort rose to Dani's lips, but then her connection with Silas snapped free. Her consciousness slammed back into her body, and the quick return left her dizzy, making her stumble.

"Careful. You're okay. Just breathe," Spencer said, grabbing hold of her elbow until the wave of dizziness passed. "Get anything useful?"

Dani relayed what Pam had said, purposefully ignoring the concerned expression Raj had plastered all over his face, like he wanted to reach for her and hated that there was no need for him with Spencer already holding her up.

"That sounds like Uncle Caleb." Spencer gently released Dani, waited a beat to make sure she was steady on her feet, then ran a hand through his hair. This time, when his fingers came away, his curls were a brilliant red. "He's not going to cooperate easily. He's a real prick."

Dani squeezed her hands into fists, her anger distracting her from the fascinating illusion magic the reformed necromancer seemed to be using. "I'm sure I can make him bleed easily enough. Where do we find him?"

Spencer rattled off an address on the south end of Blackthorn. "Don't tell him I sent you," he said, turning back to his now bubbling concoction on the table. "I'd hate to give him an excuse for a family reunion."

"Thanks, Spence. I owe you one." Raj clapped Spencer on the back.

"I'd say this makes us even," Spencer said, but he didn't elaborate.

"I'll let you know if we have any luck with Caleb." Raj opened the door and slipped down the stairs.

Dani made to follow, but Spencer called out to her to wait. "Yeah?" She asked, one hand on the door.

"Take this," he said, handing her a bag.

"What is it?" She peered into the cloth and found a black Glock and several boxes of bullets. Dani looked at Spencer quizzically. "You know bullets don't banish demons, don't you?"

"These ones do," he said, a hint of pride coloring his inflection.

"I can't pay for these," Dani said, even as she clutched the bag to her chest.

"Consider it an advance payment." Spencer's blue eyes turned stormy. "When you see my uncle, hit him at least one extra time for me."

Dani followed Raj out to the car, the Glock and bullets clutched tight to her chest. Her mind was reeling with so many unanswered questions. There was so much history between the two men, and though it shouldn't matter, she was painfully curious. Why hadn't her mother told her that some necromancers had their power thrust upon them like an unwanted gift they couldn't return.

But Spencer gave it up.

She glanced at Raj, who was navigating the thin evening traffic. He played the part of a so-called moral necromancer, one who only made deals with willing victims, but he hadn't forsaken his heritage like Spencer had. He was still profiting off demonic deals, no matter what *line* he thought he kept.

"Do you need to stop and get anything before we visit Spencer's uncle?" Shadows played across Raj's face as the car sped under street light after street light.

Dani pulled out the gun and checked the clip. It was full, so she looked through one of the boxes of extra ammunition, loading a second clip that was in the bag. The bullets felt like they had been coated in some sort of slippery substance, and runic symbols were carved onto the side of each. Yet even with the weight of the gun in her hands, she'd feel safer with her sword.

"Yeah, take the next ri—" Pain lanced up Dani's spine, and a scream tore from her throat, echoing back at her in the small vehicle. Silas and Jasper stitched themselves back on her forearms, the pain always worse when it wasn't their choice to return. Panting, she reached blindly for Raj's arm. "Lana," she said on an exhale.

She didn't have to continue. Raj took one look at the Ink tattooed against her skin and made a hasty U-turn, speeding back toward his apartment. They rode in silence, the car screaming through intersections. Raj's strong jaw flexed as he drove, his knuckles cracking when his grip tightened on the steering wheel.

A few blocks from his house, he finally glanced at

her, his dark eyes full of concern. "Are you okay? Can you fight?"

Dani chambered a bullet in her new Glock. "Whoever hurt Silas and Jasper is going to eat lead." She considered him, remembering what happened the last time they faced the succubus in the alley. "What about you?"

"I'll be fine." He pulled into the driveway, and they both sprang from the car the second it was parked. They crept toward the front door, and Raj unlocked the door "Three . . . Two . . . " On *one*, he swung open the door, and they both rushed into the grand foyer.

Silence greeted them. Silence, and signs of a struggle.

Chairs were toppled over. There was blood on the marble floor.

"Poe," Dani called, and the raven pulled from the skin on Dani's chest, the sound of wings rustling on the wind filling her ears.

"Dani, look out!"

Pain exploded, hard and fast, across Dani's back. She fell forward, catching herself in a roll, and was on her feet a moment later. She turned and came face-to-face with a many-toothed demon, scales poking through its human skin. The demon growled. Dani rolled out her shoulders.

"Bring it, asshole." She sprang forward, pushing

her enhanced speed to its limit, punching the demon with all her strength. The monster's head snapped to the side, but though she was fast, the demon was faster. It swiveled right, and Dani could barely track the movement before the demon's fist buried into her side.

The air left Dani's lungs in a rush, but she caught it again on the next inhale and reached for the gun at her waistband. The demon knocked her to the ground before she could fire, and the gun skittered across the floor, leaving Dani with little more than her fists and her wits.

Glass shattered behind her. A stampede of heavy footsteps. When she managed to look up again, the room had filled with demons. A dozen, maybe more. Poe swooped and dove, talons flashing, while Raj conjured some kind of magic, his eyes glowing and fingers tracing demonic symbols that created wide, shields that looked like water in the air. He wielded them like battering rams and sent a nearby demon crashing across the room with the magical forcefield.

Focus, Danika! Poe squawked at her. *I cannot fight this many demons alone.*

Dani lashed out with a vicious rear elbow, breaking her demon's nose. The creature howled, and Dani scrambled to her feet, running for the gun. "Kiva!" she cried, gasping as the mighty panther slipped from her back, the Ink pooling against marble before coalescing into the roaring form of her most powerful Ink.

Kiva pounced on the nearest demon, giving Dani enough time to grab the gun and aim her first shot. The bullet tore from the chamber and buried itself in the forehead of a vampiric demon sneaking up behind Raj. The necromancer whirled around as the demon's blood splattered against his back. The creature fell to the ground in a heap of exorcised flesh.

"Thank you, Spencer," Dani said, adjusting her grip and shooting another demon. The bullet lodged in the monster's shoulder, but without a kill shot, it simply cried out in pain. Dani hadn't trained with guns, but her heightened senses quickly corrected her aim.

The next shot landed true, hitting the creature in the chest and sending it back to hell. Across the room, Kiva pounced on another demon, tearing out its throat with her massive teeth.

On the other side of the room, Raj was holding his own against yet another demon. They traded blows, the demon's fists glancing off Raj's shimmering, transparent shield. Raj shoved his hands forward, and his shield crashed into the demon so hard it snapped its neck. The creature crumbled to the floor, temporarily stunned.

Another demon rushed Dani, screaming and slashing at her with razor sharp nails. She dodged under the attack and kicked the creature hard in the chest. It stumbled back, and she finished it off with a bullet between the demon's eyes.

When she glanced, up, all the remaining demons lay in various states of injury on the floor, but none of them were moving. Normally, she'd decapitate the corpses to banish the demons and let Jasper or Silas consume the remains, but the heaviness in her arms told her they were still too wounded to come out. Though she hated to waste the bullets, without her sword she was forced to shoot each one to make sure they stayed down and dead—permanently this time. "Everyone okay?"

Fine, Little Hunter. Kiva licked her paws clean of blood and padded over to where Dani was holstering her now-empty gun. *Who's your friend?*

Poe let out an indignant sound. *Our Danika has been consorting with necromancers.*

"No one's consorting, Poe."

Raj shot Dani an odd look. "What?"

"It's nothing. Poe. Kiva. Return." The Ink burst into a cloud of liquid black and sliced into Dani's chest and back. "Are you okay?" Dani approached Raj carefully. Blood dripped from his nose down to his full lips.

"I'm fine." Raj wiped the blood on the back of his wrist. "It's been awhile since I used so much magic. Just a little rusty."

Dani tried not to consider where Raj acquired said magic. It was so much easier to pretend he wasn't a necromancer when the signs of his demonic deals weren't so readily apparent. She wondered how many more deals he had struck, how many more powers he kept to himself.

"If you say so," Dani said at last, surveying the scattered bodies on the floor. They were in an array of decomposition now that demonic magic wasn't keeping them animated. "Can you tell if they were raised by Spencer's uncle?"

"Not with all of them banished, no." Raj wiped at his face again, but his nose was bleeding faster than before.

"Why don't you clean yourself up. We don't want to storm Caleb's place looking like we barely escaped whatever trap this was supposed to be." Dani fought the urge to lead Raj to the sink herself. She had more important things to do than play nurse.

I told you I wanted this nonsense out of the house.

The memory of her mother's voice caught Dani off guard. It swallowed her up until she was on the other side of the country, nursing school pamphlets in her lap. Andrea thought college was a waste of time, and here Dani was, over a year later, finally agreeing with her mother. A mother who now relied on doctors and nurses to stay safe.

Dani squeezed her eyes shut against the threatening tears.

Pain exploded against the back of Dani's head. Her knees gave out beneath her. She crumbled to the floor, her vision going in and out. As the shadows closed in, Dani saw a familiar face smirking down at her.

Pam.

13

Voices filtered in first, hushed but unhurried. The rise of questions and the steady thrum of clipped answers. Next came the smell, pungent and vile, so strong Dani had to fight against the strong, self-preserving urge to gag. And then, with a violent jerk, she woke.

The rise to consciousness was sudden and overwhelming, like jumping into a frigid lake. Dani gasped, blinking against the darkness, looking for detail in the shadowed shapes before her eyes.

Thick candles lined the room, their flames jaunty and flickering. Dani took stock of her situation. Her body hurt, her head especially, but nothing felt broken. She was bound tightly, her arms chained palm up against an iron chair, her legs shackled to the floor.

The damp air was cold against Dani's bare skin, and there was far more visible than there was before. When Dani looked down, she found her shirt in ribbons. *Not ribbons,* she realized. Whoever had taken her had cut away the places where her Ink marked her, exposing the intricate black designs that made up Poe's tattoo.

They knew who she was. *What* she was.

Fear climbed up her ribs like they were the rungs of a jungle gym. It nestled around her heart and lungs, festering, making it hard to breathe.

"Ooh, looks like someone's finally awake." Lana—no, not Lana, *Pam*—walked into view. The succubus trailed a finger across Dani's exposed collarbone. "We could have had so much fun when you tied me up." Pam settled herself in Dani's lap and kissed her cheek. "But you had to make it all boring."

Dani reached for a biting retort, but when she tried to speak, she realized her mouth was gagged. As fresh terror panicked her lungs—if Dani couldn't speak, she couldn't summon the Ink to her aid—two men stepped forward. They wore black robes that billowed around them. The taller of the two had a shaved head, yet even that couldn't hide the resemblance to curly-haired Spencer. This must be his uncle. The one who summoned Pam.

"Are you sure this is the Carrier?" the shorter of the men asked, glancing from Pam to Caleb.

"Of course, I'm sure." Pam pouted and slipped from Dani's lap. She approached the younger necromancer and trailed a finger down his face. He shuddered but kept his vision forward, not looking at her directly. The succubus glanced over her shoulder at Dani. "Aren't my minions adorable?"

When Dani didn't reply, Pam flounced away, dancing to music only she could hear. The moment her back was turned, Caleb struck the other necromancer hard across the face. "Don't you dare question our lady's judgment. We serve at her pleasure."

The younger man shrank back, bowing his head. "I'm sorry. It's just the Carrier. . . she's younger than I expected."

"Finish the potion," Caleb snapped, pointing to the other side of the room, where a trio of similarly robed figures bent over a bubbling pot. "We don't have all night."

"As you wish." The man bowed and slipped back to the other side of the room. He reached for a wooden spoon and stirred the foul-smelling liquid counterclockwise.

Dani strained to see the faces of the other necromancers across the room. Was Raj among their ranks? Had he betrayed her? She was a fool to think she could trust him. Her mother never would have fallen for his quick smile and kind words.

A small explosion rocked the room, the blast knocking Dani's teeth together. Pam stumbled as the ground shook, but she righted herself and danced over to Dani. "Isn't this exciting? I haven't had this much fun since my first orgy in 1301. I think I was in Greece. It's so hard to keep track of your human geography."

"Lady Pamela," the young necromancer from before said with a pious bow, "we're ready."

Pam clapped her hands and kissed the young man. His face burned scarlet, and when Caleb cleared his throat behind them both, the shorter necromancer bowed and stepped away. Behind him, the trio of other necromancers used thick gloves to carry the bubbling cauldron toward Dani.

They set the cast iron legs carefully on the ground, and the putrid smell nearly made Dani gag. She swallowed down the reflex, but a terrible fear made her entire body tremble. She pulled against her restraints as Caleb picked up a thick wooden spoon and dipped it into the boiling liquid.

"Ooh, what'll that do?" Pam asked, hanging on the young necromancer again, letting her fingers trail up and down his chest.

Caleb flashed her a wicked grin, but he still bowed

his head before speaking. "It'll burn those wretched spirits from her skin. They'll never trap you again, my lady."

No! Dani struggled against her restraints, frenzied with panic. She pulled and pulled and pulled, but the chains simply rattled against the chair, unbroken. The Ink stirred against her skin, but without her voice to set them free, they were trapped.

Spencer's uncle pulled the wooden spoon from the cauldron. Bits of the liquid slipped to the floor, the stone hissing as it burned away. "Where shall I start?"

Pam chewed at her lip, considering. Finally, she pointed at Silas, the python wrapped around Dani's right forearm. "That one," she said with a dramatic pout. "It nearly bit me."

Dani fought against the gag in her mouth—begging, pleading, tears rolling down her cheeks—but none of her words would fully form. She pulled harder against her restraints. The cuffs and chains bit into her skin, but she couldn't break free. Caleb lowered the ladle toward her right arm . . .

And poured the boiling liquid over her skin.

The scream that tore from Dani's throat wasn't human. It was the keening death cry of a centuries old being. The liquid burrowed into her skin, eating away flesh and Ink. As the last of her skin melted away, the python's form pulled free, Silas solidifying just enough for his eyes to find hers. *Dani . . .*

His wild, terrified screams filled the room to bursting as the potion carved his soul from hers, leaving only jagged, torn edges behind.

Then— Silence.

Silas was suddenly gone, and Dani felt his absence like a hole in her heart. Felt it in the weakening of her muscles and softening of her bones. Her lungs didn't fill as full. Her eyes less clear. Finally, her ears adjusted to the loss of Silas's scream, and the gurgle of the bubbling potion grew loud again. Her shuddered gasps audible and broken and horrible.

Pam cringed. "That looks disgusting."

Dani followed the demon's gaze. At first, she didn't recognize the red, blistered thing before her. Then, with a twist of her stomach, she realized it was her arm. Her fingers trembled, and her entire arm was slick with blood.

She looked up, rage and loss and hurt burning away the last remnants of fear. Pam flinched, and Dani tucked her thumb into her palm and *pulled.*

Her hand, now slippery with her insides exposed to the elements, slid free of the cuff. More skin tore, but it was nothing compared to the pain she'd already experienced. Dani grabbed the gag and pulled it from her mouth, tasting the tang of blood on her lips.

"Kiva," she called, breathless from grief and hoarse from the screams that had ripped past her lips. The panther burst from her back, and Dani didn't even register the pain before Kiva's roars shook the basement room.

"Poe. Jasper. Si—" Dani cut herself off as she tried to summon Silas, and grief slammed into her again. He was *gone*. Forever. She screamed again, this time a sound full of fury and the promise of death, as Poe and Jasper burst from her body.

Poe dove at Caleb, talons flashing, and Kiva gripped the chains in her mighty jaws and snapped the metal, freeing Dani from the chair. Dani rushed the young necromancer currently aiming a dagger at Jasper, catching him around the ribs and pummeling him into the ground near the cauldron. She hit the hooded man again and again and again until his eyes rolled back in his head. Dani stood and grabbed the cauldron, not caring that the metal seared her palms, and tipped the boiling contents over the man.

The necromancer screamed, and she screamed with him. His pain and her rage filled the room as the potion slipped past the man's lips and boiled his lungs.

"Stay away from here," Dani called to the remaining Ink, gesturing to the pool spreading underneath her boots. "Understood?"

We must hurry, Danika, Poe snapped at her, and the comfort of his usual bossy attitude nearly had Dani in tears. *There are more.*

Before Dani could ask what exactly there was more of, the cellar door burst open and wild demons and robed necromancers stormed down the stairs.

A demon rushed Dani, fangs protruding past its lower lip. She ducked and used her subsequent upward momentum to power a vicious uppercut that caught the monster beneath the chin. It staggered back, right into Kiva's jaws. Her fangs sank into his shoulder, puncturing his chest. The demon shuddered and fell still.

"Dani!"

The voice echoed everywhere around her, but she couldn't place which of the Ink called to her. The voice came again, louder and more insistent this time, and she realized it wasn't inside her head. It was coming from further in the basement.

She glanced back at the fray, hesitant to leave. "Do you have this?" she asked Kiva, who was prowling before her as Jasper grew to at least twenty feet long and wrapped tight around one of the necromancers, squeezing the life from her body.

We have it covered, child. Go.

"Don't kill Pam. Lana's still in there. And don't let Jasper eat Caleb," Dani called and took off toward the sound of her name. At the far end of the cellar, a small hallway branched off to the right. She squeezed through, wishing she had more than her fists and her fury as weapons.

When the hall opened up, she found a series of cells. The center cage was the only occupied one in the room, and on the other side of the bars was Raj.

"Oh, thank god," he said, crumbling against the bars. "You're alive."

Dani stalked toward the cell, her arm burning with unbearable pain now that adrenaline wasn't pumping so thoroughly through her system. "God had nothing to do with it." When she got close, she noticed the blood on Raj's clothes. The bruising already coloring his warm brown skin. The swelling around his eye. "You look like hell."

Raj ignored the poisoned barb in her voice. "You have to let me out."

"Why?" Dani tried to cross her arms, but the pain made her cry out. Her wounds weren't healing, not fast enough.

"What happened?" Raj looked her over, his gaze catching on her bloody arm. "What did they do to you?"

Dani stepped away, suddenly wary. She didn't have any of the Ink there to back her up. Was this all an act? Another trap? A failsafe in case their first plan fell through?

"Let me help you, Dani. Please." Raj reached through the bars. "Give me your hand."

Slowly, cautiously, she approached the cell. She raised her ruined arm as high as she could, and Raj caught the back of her wrist and supported her arm's weight. "This might feel weird," he said, but he didn't give Dani time to question him. His eyes glowed white, and her burned skin went cool and started stitching itself back together.

Before her arm was fully healed, Raj cried out and dropped her wrist. Angry blisters had formed along his skin, in the same places her burns had been.

"You can heal?" Dani asked, incredulous. "How?"

"Long story." Raj grit his teeth and clutched his arm to his chest. "You have to let me out. There are dozens of demons here. You won't be able to fight them all on your own."

Dani felt herself hesitate, but she looked from her arm to his, at the pain he'd willingly absorbed from her. "Where are the keys?"

Raj pointed to a little nook in the wall behind her. "I think they put everything there."

Dani approached the shelving carved into the stone wall. While she didn't see any keys, a beautiful sight glinted back at her. The Glock.

"Stand back," she said and slid the second clip she'd loaded earlier into the gun.

"No. Wait!"

She fired, the bullet shattering the lock on the cell. Raj flinched away and cautiously stepped out once he realized he was still in one piece. He moved gingerly, his body more badly beaten than Dani had first guessed.

"Are you sure you can fight?"

Raj turned and traced a pattern in the air, drawing another of his demonic shields. He shoved his hands forward, and his magic crushed the cells.

"Why the hell couldn't you do that before?"

"There were wards inside the cells," he said, turning and limping quickly down the hallway back toward the main room where the Ink still fought the onslaught of demons and necromancers. "I tried everything to get free when I heard you scream."

Tears blurred Dani's vision, and she hurried past Raj so he wouldn't see. In her haste, she was the first to emerge into the main part of the basement. The floor was littered with demons and necromancers, and Jasper was currently halfway through consuming what looked like the remains of a nightmare demon, its black talons still visible near its waist. Poe sat on Caleb's still chest while Kiva prowled before a cornered Lana.

"Huh," Raj said, resting against the wall. "I guess you don't need me after all."

"Guess not," Dani agreed, but there was no malice in her words. The only emotion left in her was a bottomless well of grief. Silas should be there, fighting Jasper over the nightmare demon. Those were always his favorite. He said they tasted minty.

Dani kneeled before Spencer's uncle, and a cold wave of power shivered through her when he stared back with unadulterated fear.

Still, he played at bravery. "You'll pay for this," he said, even as his voice trembled. "She will stop you."

"Who, Pam?" Dani glanced at the succubus, who kept trying to pet Kiva, despite the way the panther snapped at her hand each time. "Not once I take this."

Dani shoved her fingers into Caleb's eye socket. Her blood-soaked fingers struggled to grip the slimy orb as Caleb thrashed beneath her, but she finally found the base and tore with all her strength.

Her stomach clenched as the cluster of nerves and connective tissue ripped away, but Dani let grief wash away any guilt over harming someone who was technically human. She stood with Caleb's eye clutch gently in her hand while the man screamed and writhed on the floor, clutching his face. "Think this will work for the amulet?"

Raj nodded, looking a little queasy. "It should."

"Great." She stood and pointed at Pam. "Let's go." Kiva led them all up the stairs, Poe riding on her shoulders, still breathing heavily.

"I like this one," Pam said, still trying to burying her hands in Kiva's fur. "Come here, kitty."

Kiva growled and snapped her jaws. Jasper, finished with his demon, let out a moan and burst into Ink, wrapping back around Lana's left arm, too full to move.

Tears stung at Dani's eyes as she took in the contrast between her arms. Her left bearing Jasper's form, the right now scabbed over, a mottled graveyard where Silas once lived. She blinked the emotion away, forcing herself to swallow it down.

She still had work to do.

14

Dani sat at Raj's kitchen counter, nursing a glass of scotch. In a shining crystal wine glass, Caleb's hastily extracted eyeball waited for his nephew Spencer to arrive. Dani glanced at it between sips of the amber liquid, trying to fortify her frayed nerves. The ex-necromancer had asked her to hit his uncle, but that didn't mean he wanted Dani to rip off body parts.

"I can offer you anything," a once-sultry voice begged from behind her. "*Anything*. Don't do this. Please."

"You have nothing I want, demon." Dani peered over her shoulder. The succubus had worked steadily through the stages of grief, her anger finally giving way to bargaining.

"Ignore her," Raj said, returning after a quick pop

upstairs to shower and change. The blood had washed away, but the bruising remained. Dani's gaze lingered over the fresh white bandages on his forearm, where he'd absorbed some of her pain to help speed along her own healing. She wondered what he bargained away for the ability to heal others at the expense of hurting himself.

The more she learned about Raj, the more questions she had. And the more she realized the image she had of necromancers—an image that looked a lot like Caleb, actually—was far from the whole truth of who they were.

Raj stopped on the other side of the kitchen island and poured himself a drink, tossing it back with a hiss. "She'll be gone soon enough."

"But I know things," Pam insisted. "I can help you fight the underworld! I know more about demons than a hundred necromancers could ever hope to know." She paused, and Dani could feel the demon's gaze on her back. "I could teach *him* how to make your toes curl in bed."

Despite the concerned—and more than a little embarrassed—look Raj gave her, Dani swiveled to face the succubus. "Can you bring back Silas?" she asked, her tone flat.

Pam's lower lip trembled. "He's gone. There's no bringing him back."

"Then you have nothing I want."

"Sorry I'm late!" A moment later, Spencer came careening around a corner, his dark curls—back to their original deep blue—lay in a haphazard mess on his head. He sat a still-bubbling vial on the counter. "This stuff does *not* travel easily. Do you have the blood?"

Dani knocked against the counter next to the wineglass. "Will this work?"

Spencer's gaze traveled from Dani's hand to the torn eyeball, and he let out a low chuckle. "Remind me to never get on your bad side." He picked up the glass and tipped it over his potion, the eyeball flopping this way and that as it rolled down the bowl and landed with a hiss in the potion.

"How can you even do all this?" Dani asked, watching as the liquid consumed Caleb's eye. The potion glowed a soft pink. "I thought you gave up being a necromancer?"

"I did," Spencer agreed, pulling a golden charm from his pocket. "I knew I wanted to leave, but I hadn't had the courage to tell my parents before my eighteenth birthday. I had to summon a demon and claim another power, so I chose something I could take with me."

Spencer paused and dipped the gold charm into the jar. Almost like a straw, the amulet sucked up the viscous liquid until it had all been absorbed into the gold. "That ritual left me an alchemist of sorts."

"I . . . don't have any idea what that means in this context."

"Magic is kind of like science to me now. If I study something long enough, I can recreate it without begging for help from a demon. Not everything, of course, but my family *hates* it, which more than makes up for its limitations." Spencer grinned and pulled the amulet from the now-empty jar. "That should do it!" When he looked up to hand the locket to Dani, he finally looked at them. *Really* looked. "What the hell happened to you two?"

"Your uncle happened." Dani snatched the amulet from Spencer, but he wrapped his fingers around her wrist. Her *bad* wrist. His gaze traveled up her arm, the wound now a patchwork of raised red scars, and when he finally met her eyes, there was something close to pity there. "I don't want to talk about it," she said, unable to stop the hitch in her voice.

"You don't have to," Spencer soothed, pulling her off the stool and into a fierce hug. "I'm so sorry."

Dani sank into his embrace, allowing herself a moment of warmth, allowing all her pain to bubble up to the surface. As Spencer held her, she realized she couldn't remember the last time someone touched her like this, the last time someone offered comfort with no strings attached. Loneliness threatened to crush her, but she forced herself to pull away. She had a job to do. On the other side of the island, Raj watched her carefully, his expression schooled into a neutrality he clearly didn't feel.

"Well then," she said, clearing her throat. "Let's get this over with."

The succubus wailed and begged as Dani approached. Promised to bring her riches, make her body sing, grant her any power she could dream up. As Dani raised the amulet to place the chain around Lana's neck and give the woman control of her body again, Pam raised her hands. "Your mother!" she cried, the words stalling Danika's hands. "I can help you find the demon who hurt her."

Fresh pain stirred inside Dani's already broken heart. The past few days were the first time since the attack she'd been able to focus on anything besides the demon that ruined her life. She would have given anything to find that monster and rip his head from his shoulders.

"You can?"

"Of course, darling. Demons are such gossips. There's no way whoever tampered with your mother's mind would be able to keep their mouth shut about it. Taking out a Carrier is worth decades of bragging rights."

She was tempted, so fucking tempted, to say yes. To let the succubus take over Lana completely to save her own mother. But Dani thought of Cassie, of the young girl's worry over her big sister.

Dani couldn't destroy their family, even if it meant she might never get her own back.

"I don't need your help," Dani said at last and fastened the amulet around Lana's throat.

The woman's head fell back against the chair. Her body trembled and fell still. Then Lana, the *real* Lana, looked up. "What did you do?" she said, breathless. "What about Cassie?"

"Cassie will be fine," Dani promised. "Your deal with the succubus isn't broken. She's still here, still inside of you. But now *you* get to drive."

"Come with me," Raj said, stepping forward like he'd promised. "I'll take you to your sister."

Lana nodded, still dazed and a bit unsteady on her feet. Dani and Spencer trailed them to the front door, where Lana paused, panicked. "What about my job? How am I supposed to take care of Cassie?" She started to spiral right before them, increasingly panicked worries falling off her lips.

"You'll figure it out." Dani laid her hands on Lana's shoulders in a gesture she hoped was soothing. "The important thing is that Cassie's going to be okay. You'll be there to take care of her and watch her grow up. You'll get to argue about what shows you watch and ground her when she tries to sneak out when she's a little older. You have your family back, Lana. Everything else will fall into place."

Lana reached up squeezed Dani's hands, tears sparkling in eyes that matched her young sister's blue irises. "Thank you. For everything."

"It's what I do." But Dani's broken heart warmed all the same.

The four of them climbed into Raj's car and made the quick drive to Lana's house. Dani texted Cassie to tell her she was coming over, but she didn't mention Lana. She wanted it to be a surprise.

Cassie was waiting on her front porch when they arrived, sitting on the top step.

Before Raj could even shift the car into park, Lana flung open her door and raced up the driveway. Cassie burst into tears when she saw her big sister, standing in time to be crushed in Lana's hug.

Raj finally got the car in park, and Dani climbed out, leaning against the hood. She could feel Kiva's approval purring through her, and she imagined Poe reluctantly admitting that his earlier assessment had been wrong. She'd saved Lana and Cassie both.

Silas would be proud.

Dani's eyes filled with tears, so she didn't notice Cassie's approach until her thin arms were wrapped tight around Dani, hugging her. "Thank you," the younger girl said, over and over, a mantra of gratitude that only made Dani cry harder.

Lana made them stay for food, whipping up the best damn vegan pancakes Dani had ever had. The sisters loved Spencer, who regaled them with embarrassing stories of the antics he and Raj pulled as kids. Dani was positive he manipulated the stories to hide the demonic parts of their shared past, but she did her best to put on a brave face and laughed along with them anyway.

Raj smiled, but he kept shooting worried glances at Dani. And when she excused herself to the bathroom—where she also borrowed Lana's face wash and scrubbed away some of the grime and grief of the evening—she found Raj waiting for her in the hall.

"What did Pam mean," he asked, his voice achingly gentle. "When she said she could help your mother?"

The question caught Dani off guard. She glanced down the hall to the dining room, where laughter and life spilled out. She wanted to be there with them, not reliving more of her grief with Raj.

But he had helped her. Without him—and through him, Spencer—this reunion wouldn't be possible. And maybe it was the hole in her soul that had belonged to Silas or the grief over losing a lead to her mother's cure, but some small part of her wanted to tell him. Wanted to rip open her heart and let it bleed, if only to see if he'd help stitch it back together.

So, she told him. Not everything, not even close, but she told him that there had been an attack. That her mother's mind was no longer her own. That Dani was all alone in the world.

"Except for the Ink," he said, reaching for her hands. "You still have them."

"Not all of them," she whispered back, fighting the rising tide of her tears.

"You have me." Raj pulled her close, tucking her head under his chin. "And Spence."

The absurdity of it all made her laugh. Her only allies in Blackthorn were a disgraced former necromancer and the head of the Dasari clan. Men she'd known barely a day yet could already feel the beginnings of trust starting to stitch between them.

They left soon after, Raj dropping her off at her apartment before bringing Spencer back to his place. She waved as they drove away, cringing when her building's front door whined as she yanked it open.

Half-way up the stairs, her phone rang. She answered, and Frank's booming filled the hall, chewing her out for missing her shift. Dani let him scream, and when she reached her apartment and pulled out her keys.

"You know what, Frank? Shove your shitty, under-paid job up your ass. I quit."

Relief flooded through her when she hung up. She'd have to find some other way to pay for her mother's care, but first, there were more pressing concerns.

She and the Ink needed space to grieve.

15

Dani's apartment was the cleanest it had ever been. After she'd scrubbed herself clean of the hellish night, showering as quickly as she could under the still-cold water, she'd washed every surface until the dingy metal appliances and chipped vinyl countertops gleamed. She pushed her body to exhaustion, but Silas deserved nothing less.

When there was nothing more to clean and she'd lit every candle she owned to provide light in her dark apartment, she called the Ink.

Kiva appeared first, and Dani sank into her warmth. She hugged Kiva tight, burying her face in the panther's fur. Kiva didn't say anything, but she didn't need to: Dani could feel the sorrow radiating off her. And though she had braced for it, there wasn't any of the blame or reproach she was expecting.

If she was honest with herself, Dani knew it wasn't Kiva she had to worry about throwing the night's horrors back in her face. She had Poe for that.

The raven answered her call swiftly, coming to rest on top of the fridge, his feathered head cocked to one side. Watching. Waiting.

"Go ahead, Poe. Let me have it." Dani forced herself to let go of Kiva, and she stood tall beneath Poe's watchful eye, awaiting his judgment.

But Poe chirped at her and swooped down from the fridge, landing on her shoulder. *This wasn't your fault, Danika.* He nuzzled his beak against her chin. *You don't bear any blame for this, love.* Poe's voice was choked with emotion. *I should have warned you. Trained you better. It was my job to protect all of you.*

"It's not your fault," she said through fresh tears. "You told me to get rid of Pam. If I had only listened—"

Kiva nudged Dani's hip with her head. *You brought that family back together, young one. Do not diminish the good of what you've done.*

Dani nodded, but she examined the now white scars on her forearm instead of looking at either of them. Part of her wished the wound had taken longer to heal. She deserved to feel the pain linger. She wanted proof of the freshness of her grief. "I don't know if I can face Jasper," she whispered. Already his pain was overwhelming her senses. She didn't know if she could bear to hear that same hurt in his voice.

He needs your strength. He needs all of us. Kiva licked Dani's scars, her tongue warm and rough against the raised, puckered skin. *Let him out.*

She whispered his name, tears claiming her as his grief pulled away from her body, leaving her personal pain behind.

Dani collapsed on her mattress and pulled her knees into her chest. "I'm so sorry, Jasper. So, *so* sorry." It was getting hard to breathe, her heart racing so fast she was afraid she might pass out.

Jasper didn't say anything. He slithered onto the bed and wrapped his tail around the arm that once bore Silas. The king cobra's physiology didn't permit him to cry, but his grief was no less heavy. Kiva climbed into bed with them, curling up behind Dani.

"Get over here, Poe," Dani said, brushing her fingers along Jasper's scales then burying her hand in Kiva's soft fur. Poe ruffled his feathers, and for a second, she thought he might refuse, but then he flew over to them and claimed a space on Kiva's shoulders.

They didn't have to say how much they'd miss Silas. It flowed through each of them, wordless but true. Poe fell asleep first, his beak coming to rest against the feathers on his chest. Dani curled up against Kiva, lifting Poe to tuck him protectively against her chest.

And finally, they slept, a pile of grief and love, bonded for life.

Dani woke to the incessant buzzing of her phone. She reached for it, but by the time she flipped it open to answer, the call was lost.

She stretched, taking in her small apartment. Kiva and Poe were still asleep, but her waking had roused Jasper. His tongue flicked out, tasting the air, and Dani couldn't remember the last time one of the snakes stayed outside her skin for an entire night. He watched her, a questioning tilt to his head, and Dani nodded.

It hurt when he burst into shadows and returned to her skin, but she had a new appreciation for the sensation. She'd never complain about that kind of pain ever again.

All her candles had burned themselves out, leaving

pools of wax on the floor and counters, but the sun was bright in the sky, light filtering in through the small window. Her phone chimed with a voicemail. Begrudgingly, she flipped it open and punched in her passcode.

"This is Blackthorn Hospital, calling for Miss Danika Frost."

Dani cursed under her breath. She was supposed to stop by the receptionist desk to make payment. They were probably hours away from kicking her mother out.

"We wanted to confirm receipt of your recent online payment," the voicemail continued. "Your next bill is due in fifteen months. We'll reach out again thirty days before payment to confirm the card we have on file."

Dani replayed the message three more times before she let herself believe it was true. Someone had paid her mother's hospital bills. But who—

It had to be Raj. He was the only one who knew about her mother's condition, but she hadn't told him which hospital she was staying in. How had he found her? *Why* had he paid for so much of her care?

Danika? Kiva's concerned voice penetrated Dani's runaway thoughts. *Is everything okay?*

"I think it is." A weight Dani hadn't realized she was carrying suddenly lifted from her chest. If she had any tears left in her body, she'd be crying again. "Someone paid Mom's bill. She's not going to get kicked out."

Poe ruffled his feathers and used his beak to lay them straight. *Excellent. Now you'll have more time for hunting.*

She couldn't help it. She rolled her eyes. "I do still have to pay rent and buy food, Poe. Money isn't optional in this world."

He harrumphed, but it was Kiva who asked what she was going to do next.

Dani didn't know. She could probably get a better waitressing job now that she had experience, but the thought of delivering trays of food to mocking high schoolers and shitty tippers threatened to burst the bubble of joy the voicemail had created.

But then she thought of Cassie. She thought of saving Lana. Of reuniting their family. Hope bloomed inside her as an idea started to take hold. "What if I could make money helping people?"

How? Poe asked, ever practical.

All of the pieces snapped together in quick succession. It was perfect.

"I'll be a private investigator," Dani said, and it sounded so right she wanted to shout it from the rooftop. "I can hunt demons and help people like Lana. The bills will get paid, I won't have to neglect my duties, and the research skills will help me find the reaper who hurt Mom."

Dani could see it now. An office of her own, her name stamped on the frosted glass. She smiled a little, imagining a python twisting along the bottom of business cards. Silas would still be part of it all, the heart of everything she did.

Before she could expand on her blossoming idea, someone knocked on the door.

Kiva growled, and Poe flew up to Dani's shoulder. *Did you forget to pay rent again?*

"I didn't forget anything," she whispered. "Rent isn't due until next week. Both of you, return."

Dani winced, and by the time she reached the door, she was alone in the apartment. She flipped open the many locks and cracked the door to glance out into the hall.

"Raj? What are you doing here?"

He held up a white paper bag in one hand and a tray with two steaming cups in the other. "Mind if I come in? I brought breakfast."

She opened the door and let him step through. Shame tried to color her face as he took in her tiny apartment, but Dani forced the emotion down. Not because she wanted to avoid it, but because she denied its accuracy. She had survived more than most. She'd lost her mother at seventeen and still had a place to call home, no matter how small and sparse it was.

When Raj turned to face her, he smiled. "Glad to see you in one piece. Coffee?"

Dani accepted the cup and drank down the burning liquid. "Thank you," she said, glancing at the white bag as her stomach growled audibly. "What's in there?"

Raj grinned. "The best bagels in Blackthorn." He set the bag on the kitchen counter and pulled out several wrapped bagels. "I wasn't sure what you liked, so I got some with butter, cream cheese, and a couple with eggs, bacon, and cheese."

Her stomach growled again, and Dani didn't even try to hide it. "Bacon. Always the bacon one."

They ate in comfortable silence, leaning against the counter, and when Dani's stomach was finally *full* for the first time in months, she studied Raj. His lip was still swollen from whatever the other necromancers had done to him, but his eyes were bright and his smile quick.

"What?" he asked, catching Dani staring.

"Why did you help me?" She thought of the voicemail from the hospital. "Why do you *keep* helping me?"

Raj raised an eyebrow at her.

"The hospital called."

His brown cheeks went ruddy. "I didn't think they'd call you so fast."

"That doesn't answer why, Raj." Dani knew she shouldn't antagonize the man who had done so much to help her, but she couldn't help it.

Raj stared at his coffee cup, his fingers playing in the steam that rose through the small opening. "I've been groomed my whole life to take over my father's business, but all that wealth and power comes at a cost. I try to run the clubs as ethically as I can, but I've never *truly* helped someone. There's always a catch, and I always get something out of it." He tucked a few loose strands of hair behind his ears. "I don't think I've ever done something truly selfless before in my life. And then I met you."

Raj finally looked at her then, something soft and wanting in his expression. "I watched you sacrifice again and again to help those girls, and you asked for nothing in return."

"It was the right thing to do." Dani's breath caught in her chest, and Raj seemed suddenly closer yet not nearly close enough.

"No one I know does anything because it's the *right thing*, Dani." He reached for her then, his soft hands circling her waist and pulling her close. "You make me want to try."

He leaned close, so close Dani could feel the heat

of him on her skin. "Paying for my mother's care so I'd want to kiss you isn't exactly selfless," she said, near breathless.

"That's not why I did it."

Dani's hands slid up his chest, coming to rest behind his neck. "But you do. Want to kiss me, that is."

Raj smiled, and it was the first time the expression had ever seemed shy on his lips. "Only if you want me to."

And even though they stood on opposite sides of the war against demons. Even though she'd barely known him a day. Even though she didn't think her mother would ever approve, Danika Frost decided she didn't care about any of that. She was just a girl who liked a boy who liked her back.

She pulled him close and kissed him.

COMING APRIL 7th 2020!

The first full length book in the Danika Frost series is coming this spring!

Pre-order your copy now:

https://books2read.com/u/bpOp06

Thank you for reading CHOSEN! If you enjoyed the book, we would greatly appreciate it if you could consider adding a review on your bookstore of choice.

Reviews make a huge difference to the success or failure of a book, especially for newer writers like us. The more reviews a book has, the more people are likely to take a shot on picking it up. The review need only be a line or two, and it really would make the world of difference for me if you could spare the three minutes it takes to leave one.

With all our thanks,

Connor and Charlotte

9 781912 382170